Hurra

THE FIRST CHILDREN

By

Peter J Flores

This is a work of fiction. Names, characters, places and incidents either are the product of the author's imagination or are used fictitiously.

Any resemblance to actual events locales organizations or persons living or dead is entirely coincidental and beyond on the intent of the Author

ISBN **978-1540727473**

Imprint of New Atlantic Industries

To my parents, Andrea Andrews Flores Canales and Pedro E. Flores. My sisters, Victorine Canales Trevino and Janet Canales Manriquez.

CHAPTER ONE

He opened his eyes and stared at the dimly lit ceiling.

What had awaken him? He couldn't remember a dream, much less one as unpleasant as to cause him waking up. That's the way dreams are. One minute you're asleep, then when you wake, you have trouble remembering what it was all about. So vivid in a dream state, then, poof! All memory is erased. It couldn't have been a nightmare he was sure. And, he smiled, it wasn't nature calling.

He turned his head. His wife was there, sleeping peacefully it would seem. She was not the cause of his awakening and whatever the cause, it had not affected her.

He sat up.

Then he saw them, at the foot of the bed. Small, they barely topped the level of his blanket. Pale, light skinned and large black eyes--Oh, no! Not that. Exactly like one of those tabloid pictures of aliens from a UFO!

He rubbed his eyes and then pinched his forearm. It wasn't a dream. A spasm started in his stomach, actually the beginning of a laugh, because it must be a joke. There had to be someone lying on the floor manipulating these two puppets in order to play a joke on him. Carl, Sylvia or Oscar seemed the likely suspects. It was just like them although he couldn't remember when they had ever picked him as a target for one of their jokes.

But the puppets didn't move. In fact, there was no movement or sound.

He threw the blanket aside and swung his feet to the floor. Standing there, six feet tall, looking at his visitors. Still they didn't move.

He took a couple of steps to the foot of the bed. Now he had a complete view of them. Complete that is, only what he could distinguish from the poor lighting that came from a window.

Children?--No. They were the size of an eight or nine year old, four feet, maybe a few inches above that. They were either naked or wore a one-piece suit or coveralls, that seemed to have no end or beginning. Besides the large black eyes, they also had large pointy ears and a triangular looking face and very little neck.

And there was no one lying on the floor manipulating them. Manipulate what? They hadn't moved.

Then suddenly, it was quiet no longer. "John! John! It's Martin. Come to the cave. Bring the Children."

Then the creatures vanished.

His mouth open in surprise, he staggered back, the back of his knees hitting the edge of the mattress. Falling on the bed.

His wife stirred, mumbled some unintelligible sounds, and then subsided.

He didn't notice her, but laid on the bed, staring at the blank ceiling, remembering the voice. The voice of a dead man.

He sat again. Who--Where had it come from? From those creatures? He could have sworn they never opened their mouths. Not that they seem to have much of one.

Getting up again and searched the house, but they were gone. The doors and windows were locked, the ashes in the fireplace were undisturbed. He saw no one and heard not a sound--but then, they had never made any--except for that voice. Had they been the ones who had spoken? He remembered what he had read of similar experiences, they were all over the tabloids--thought transference. It couldn't be a coincidence that he had heard the words while they were there. There had to be a connection. And words from a dead man?

Not far away, another awoke to glorious sunshine. For some reason, his bones ached like they never had before. He stretched, swiveled his head, hearing the crackling of bone or was it ligament? He wasn't a doctor, not that kind anyway. He knew only what he heard and what he felt. How long had he slept? That must be it. When all you had to do was wait, you spent too much time sleeping.

There was nothing stirring. Where was the stock? Predators? That was what he was afraid of. There were still some around. He had to round up the stock. A one-man roundup, he smiled. Unless they came. Where were they?

He took several steps into the brush area and was stopped as he observed the narrow trail of crushed vegetation. Following it, he saw on bare ground the imprint of vehicle tires.

He was startled by this unexpected find. Where had they come from? How could he not have known? If they were friends, why had he not been contacted? Were they hostile?

If so, they had not bothered him, or perhaps they had not searched far enough. Yes, they would not have known he was here. But who? Who was there left to view as an enemy?

He turned to retrace his steps. For the first time he had a full view of the entrance. He stopped, mouth open. It was not as it should have been. A change had been made and he had never been aware of it. Something was wrong.

CHAPTER TWO

The city of Stonecliff had been reborn after its catastrophic demise two years earlier. True to his promise, the President of the United States and The Congress had, for once, made good on their promises. They had to. A military weapon experiment had gone awry and obliterated parts of Arizona, New Mexico and Utah. Casualties were over two hundred thousand. The only survivors were from Stonecliff, the Class of '05' holding a reunion in a sub-basement of their school. The attention of the whole world had been focused on this tragedy by a voracious media. And when the survivors were finally discovered, they had become instant media darlings. With all this publicity, the politicians had no recourse but to join in the celebration of their rescue--and pay for the misdeeds of their weapon research.

The U.S. Army Corp of Engineers had come in to do what was necessary, including opening roads, building an airport, building bridges and containing streams from flooding. In fact, just about every agency of the government had become involved. It had reimbursed or granted low interest loans to the survivors for the building of homes and businesses.

A home had been built for each surviving family. A hospital was built and Dr. Walter Heerlson, one of the survivors, put in charge. The supermarket and western store now owned by Dorothy Fenzer was partly open. It had belonged to her father and now she was running it with the help of her husband Jim Fenzer. Jim was an archaeologist and that was one skill unnecessary for rebuilding a town. Overall construction was under the direction of Aaron Sherland, another survivor, who owned several construction companies.

A school was also under construction and was being run by more survivors, Sylvia Umbrall, Carl Umbrall, Esther Bonococci and Linda Sherland.

A still unexplained consequence of the catastrophe was the failure of any children being born to any of the survivors. It had taken about a year and a half afterward that it had come to light after several wives had complained to Dr. Heerlson of their inability to conceive. It wasn't long after, that the doctor made the connection and the common denominator was the secret weapon experiment.

Reporting to the U. S. Health Services had brought an investigating team headed by Dr. Laura Criden. Another assigned to the town was Jeff Randall, special representative for Congressman Truman Sawyer, in whose district Stonecliff was located. The congressman, like most representatives, spent the majority of their time in Washington and made as few visits as possible to their respective districts. However, the eyes of the nation and the world had focused on this part of the United States and the congressman had deemed it necessary to keep himself in the public eye. Jeff Randall's job was to do just that.

The media was also not to be undone. During the past two years, numerous stories and articles had been published or appeared on the visual media. Of late though, attention had subsided while other major news events had blossomed. Nevertheless, the inhabitants knew there would be news updates as the community struggled to start a new life.

Keeping in mind there might be stringers about who were all too eager to notify the news people of any event, real or imagined, Dr. Criden took special precautions to gather the survivors in one of the makeshift classrooms. It was evening when it was less likely to be many people abroad. The old Stonecliff had rolled up the streets at dusk. The new one was no different.

The forty three survivors represented almost the entire permanent population of the town. The rest was made of government officials, construction workers and other transient personnel who were in and out almost daily.

Four of the survivors had left after the rescue to be with relatives in other parts of the country. All four had eventually returned as if drawn back by some invisible force. The catastrophe had pulled them together until they now regarded themselves as one huge family. They had been together as classmates, now they were together to rebuild the town of their birth.

Now Dr. Criden surveyed her audience before she made her presentation. In return, the audience had their look of her. Not that she was a stranger. She had talked to and examined everyone in the few months she had been here. And she wasn't hard to look at. Dark hair, brown eyes, slim, five foot seven, altogether an attractive if not pretty young lady. The final stamp of approval was the whistles of the construction workers.

Sylvia and Esther who liked to pin movie star names on their acquaintances, immediately went into gear at first meeting.

"Sandra Bullock," said Esther.

"Naw, no way," Sylvia replied. "Courtney Cox."

"All right, I'll settle for Sandra Cox.

"Now, that Jeff Randall--definitely Mel Gibson."

"Yeah, right," Sylvia for once agreed. "Mel should be happy to look like Jeff because he would gain about three, four inches towards the ceiling."

With those comments, Jeff didn't need physical description. And thus agreed, the two women embarked on a campaign to match Jeff with Dr. Laura.

Unfortunately, the doctor refused the challenge, classifying him as a Washington Toady, carpet bagger and other unkind names.

Tonight as she prepared to talk to the survivors, she was somewhat distraught since what she had to say was not what they wanted to hear. To make matters worse, she saw that Washington parasite sitting with the Umbralls and the Bonococcis. She had invited only the survivors, but, of course, there was no prohibition against bringing guests if they so desired.

"I'm not one for making long preambles or introductory speeches guaranteed to put you to sleep, then two hours later I hit you with the punch line. So I will risk sounding harsh or insensitive and give it to you straight.

"Of the forty three patients tested, all but two are sterile. All tests, samples and specimens have been sent to Atlanta for further testing. But as of right now, I don't see there shall be any reversals of the results.

"What, specifically caused this, we don't know and perhaps never shall, given the penchant Washington has of not accepting blame or responsibility. Generally, of course, it was the weapon exploding over Stonecliff that caused this condition for the inhabitants. That is the common denominator. What we need to know, what we need to get is the composition of this weapon. What chemicals or compounds were used or whether they combined with something in the area to form some toxic or deadly compound."

The audience was silent, no doubt stunned by the news. Then it was followed by a low murmur to a partner sitting alongside.

"Any questions?"

"Yes, who are these two people that escaped this calamity?" Sylvia asked.

"I'm sorry. It's confidential, but the two people shall be told later. It shall be their decision to make it public if they so wish."

"So, it's irreversible?" Dorothy asked.

"I don't want to say that," Laura grimaced. "I'm just

one doctor. Everyone should have a second opinion. That's why I sent the results to Atlanta. It could be temporary or it could be permanent. Perhaps fertility drugs could change that. As of now, I don't know.

"And I'm sorry I had to break it to you like this, but I don't believe in keeping patients in the dark about their conditions. Just be aware but don't give up hope."

"Doctor, Congressman Sawyer shall be informed of this and I shall press him to contact the Pentagon or whatever agency has control of this weapon and have them report the makeup of this weapon for medical testing," Jeff Randall spoke up from the audience.

"You're an optimist, Mr. Randall," the doctor replied, almost with a sneer. "The weapon has already been given the highest classified rating, so it's not likely they will cave in to a mere congressman. Especially one who doesn't have a seat in an important committee with the clout to impress the Pentagon."

"You may be right, Doctor," Jeff conceded. "Certainly there are precedents enough to back your statement. But I like and believe in these people here with whom I've lived for the past few months. I've made friends that I hope will last a lifetime. So I'm not going to quit trying to do something for them from the political side. If I fail, it won't be because I didn't try."

"I'm not giving up either, Mr. Randall," Laura flared out. "I've been here just as long as you have and I have just as much regard for them as you have--And I've also made friends for life. So, don't try to upstage me, sir."

"I'm not trying to fight you, Doctor," Jeff replied. "On the contrary, you threw the first punch, but I'll keep my guard down. What I'm saying is that we throw our punches at those responsible, not those in this room or in this town. This problem encompasses several fields. Medicine and politics are but two and there's no reason for us to step on each other's toes.

"That's all I have to say," he sat down.

Laura looked as if she wanted to continue the argument, but after a few seconds of holding her temper, she relaxed. "That's all for now. I'll talk to all of you later, individually, in groups or in a meeting like this.

"Goodnight, ladies and gentlemen." She left the podium.

"Well," Sylvia looked at Esther, "the lady is blunt."

"Yeah, too blunt. You reckon we oughta lend her a copy of 'How to Win Friends and Influence People?'"

But Sylvia was already off on a new thought. "I wonder who those two people are."

"Well, we could break into her office and look up the records."

"Where did you steal that plot from?--Oh, I know. Tune in on just about any soap opera ever made."

"It works for them."

Sylvia grimaced. "Cliched, contrived and coincidental, that's soap opera land.

"Let's go home and see what's on the late show."

"Wait! You forget. We have husbands now."

"Why did you have to remind me? A spinster all my life, then I finally get married and now I'm sterile. Is there some irony here?"

"No, dear, it's called a conspiracy, aimed only at you."

CHAPTER THREE

Jim and Dorothy Fenzer entered the doctor's office and were surprised to find John and Jean Edleman in the waiting room.

Dorothy pulled up short. "Didn't expect to see you two."

"Same here," said Jean. "She wanted to see us at ten this morning."

Jim nodded. "And us too, same time."

"And there's no other patients," John added.

"She has no other patients," said Dorothy. "We, our class, are her career project."

"Oh no!" exclaimed Jean. "Do you suppose..."

"The Gruesome Twosome as Sylvia might say," laughed Jim.

"My God! Is that what you think?" Jean put her hand to her mouth.

Further speculation was cut short as Dr. Criden opened her inner office door.

"Won't you come in? All of you." They went in and

saw four chairs in a semi-circle in front of her desk. They exchanged glances. Obviously all four had been expected at the same time.

Laura sat down and surveyed her patients. Jim was six two, brown hair, bronze skin, athletic build. Dorothy was five six, slim, dark shoulder length hair, green eyes and gorgeous legs. John was six feet, dark, lean, straight black hair, brown eyes. Jean was petite, five three, olive skinned, dark hair, brown eyes. Sylvia and Esther, who liked to pin movie star names on their friends had compared Dorothy to Jaclyn Smith or Hunter Tylo. Jean was Rita Moreno. Jim was Robert Stack and John was Oscar de la Hoya.

"I suppose you've been wondering, so without further ado, I can say you are probably correct in your speculation--of why you are here."

"We are--or rather two of us are the ones you mentioned the other night," Jim said.

She nodded.

"And," Jim continued, "with a bit of logic, we can whittle it down. It's not one couple, otherwise you would have call only that couple. Two couples says one person in each couple is the favored one--if you can call it that."

She nodded again. "Yes, and as you know, I don't believe in prolonging the inevitable. The favored ones, as you say, are you and John."

The two women took it differently. Jean with her hand to her mouth. Dorothy looked down and shook her head. John had that stoic look. Jim did not express any particular expression, but his hands were grasped together on his lap.

"So, I suppose we're here to find those extenuating circumstances that separate John and me from the others?" Jim broke the silence.

"Exactly," Laura agreed. "Perhaps we can narrow it down by finding out what and where each of you was and what you were doing, your contacts and so forth."

"The time period is easy to pinpoint," said Dorothy. "Jim and John left the rest of us on our 16th day or May 24th. Jim returned on June 16th, John a day earlier. So, for over three weeks they were separated from the rest of the class. That has to be the difference."

"In addition, after returning, John took off for another week," added Jean.

Laura nodded. "I think that narrows the time and area where or when it happened--whatever it was. It also means that the initial explosion may not be entirely responsible for the problem since both men were there for the first sixteen days. Something might have happened later that caused the sterility."

"Obviously," said John.

The doctor flushed. "Sorry, I have a tendency to categorize, put everything in the proper column, and then check the bottom line. I sometimes forget there's people around."

"All those figures represent people, Laura," Dorothy said softly. "Forty three people to be exact."

"My bedside manners may not be the best. I'm primarily a scientist."

"Don't be defensive, Laura. We're all your friends. And bedside manners is just another expression for human relationships."

"Ah," Jim interrupted. "Shall we get back to the purpose of this meeting? I think Dorothy and Jean are the proper people to interview for what happened while John and I were gone."

"It's got to be the digging to search for food and supplies," said Dorothy.

"And that's my fault," Jim broke in. "I gave them instructions to do just that just before we left."

"We dug holes all over downtown Stonecliff," Jean took up the story. "And in the process we brought up dead bodies and perishable food. We had to, otherwise we couldn't have kept digging."

"And what precautions did you take?" asked Laura.

"None at first," Jean replied. "Then Walter, Dr. Heerlson, insisted we cover our mouth and nose, then wash or bathe at the end of the workday."

"So you did that, covered up and bathed. Where did

you bathe?"

"In the river, but away from the mainstream where the current was too strong," said Dorothy.

"In calm or standing water?"

"No--well, yes, we had to wade through it to get to where the water ran a little faster, but not swift enough to sweep away someone," Dorothy remembered her experience at the water's edge with Larry Wilk.

"How about drinking water?"

"We used what we had stored at the Civil Defense Shelter. Then we took water from the river and boiled it before using."

"The food?"

"Again, what we had at the shelter, then what we dug up. But it was all canned or sealed and we cleaned it as best we could before opening it. We even washed any tools or equipment we found. Walter insisted on it."

"Very commendable," said Laura, "but probably primitive at best.

"How about living conditions? Sleeping, working, clothing, body intercourse."

"Intercourse?" Dorothy almost laughed. "I'm not aware there was any, but then it wasn't a question one asked of another. There was one married couple, the Longleys and a divorced set, the Bonococcis. The former might have, but not the latter--or at least not until the very end when certain relationships were finalized," she glanced at the others. "But even if everyone was promiscuous, I hardly think it would cause sterility."

"No, of course not," Laura's face got red.

"As for working conditions as Jean said, we dug up dead bodies and putrid food and then reburied them. The stench was unbearable. We used our hands. Our clothes got dirty and torn and we had nothing to replace them. We could rinse them out in the river, but it took a long time to dry because it was late in the evening and there was no sun during the day and it was damp and clammy. We did cut up some blankets from the shelter and made ponchos, but it was never satisfactory as far as protecting the women's modesty.

It was a Godsend when we finally found clothing in the ruins."

"How about sewage and--ah, disposable..."

Dorothy laughed. "I know what you mean. We dug more holes. Boy, did we dig holes. I don't think I'll ever see another hole without smelling the stink coming out.

"Yeah, we dug latrines, as the military calls them, for our waste. The same for garbage. All of them as far away as possible from our eating and sleeping areas and away from the river so we wouldn't contaminate it any more than it already was."

"The river was contaminated?"

"Some was readily visible, the rest was speculation since we couldn't see beneath the water. Who knows what was in it. It came rushing south carrying all the riches and dregs of civilization and the residue of Mother Nature.

"I guess we did as well as we could about our public health measures. But even in the best of times it was never perfect. And we were operating in a less than perfect environment. And without the proper tools and equipment to make it safe for society.

"Walter was ear, nose and throat, but he also was a good public health officer and ultimately, a fine surgeon."

"I'm sure," Laura sighed. "But somewhere in that epic event was that common denominator that affected all of you. It had to be the water, the food or the sanitation.

"I'll have to check and see if anyone took samples of the water, air, dirt, foliage. If they didn't, then it's probably hopeless now, two years later."

"You don't think it's continuing now, do you?" asked Jean.

"I doubt it. If it was, then Jim and your husband would also be sterile now. No, it happened then.

"But just to make sure, I'll run a test on myself and maybe a few others that came afterwards."

"So, basically we're no closer to finding the truth now and probably never will be tomorrow or next year," John gave her a grim look.

"Oh, I think we'll find it. What I can't guarantee is the

time it will take.

"So, what's your future?" Laura leaned forward. "That you'll never have children? Turn around and look at your spouse. That's the person you love and who loves you back. There are people who don't have that at all."

They were all silent. No quick reply came.

"I think that's enough for today. Just think about it. What happened then and what happens now."

CHAPTER FOUR

"Poor Laura," said Dorothy as they left her office, "She has personal problems galore."

"She has no time for fools and everyone is a potential candidate for one--in her eyes," agreed Jean. "But I like her."

She turned to Dorothy. "We need to work on her. It's a terrible waste of womanhood."

Dorothy nodded. "I think Jeff Randall likes her, but she won't let him get close."

"Not to change the subject," said Jim, "but where do we go from here."

"Do you want to go eat?" John asked. "There's only the diner where most of the construction workers eat."

"That wasn't what I was referring to, but it is lunchtime and since we don't have to get home and feed the kids--why not."

"That joke was uncalled for," said Dorothy. They walked towards the diner.

"What were you referring to?" asked Jean.

"Our status, the status of all the survivors. Do we try

those fertility drugs or adopt?"

"Do we have to decide now?" Dorothy was grim.

"Isn't it the women who keep worrying about their biological clocks?"

"We're all about 35," said Jean, "so we do have a few years to decide."

Dorothy laughed. "I just thought about something ironic. Martin said we were the 'First Children' that would survive a world-ending catastrophe to repopulate the world."

"Yes," Jim stared off in the distance. "Martin told us many things. But we soon found out that the world didn't end and none of us can populate their own home, much less the world."

They reached the diner and went in. It was 11:30, so they were a half hour ahead of the noonday rush. They easily found a table.

"Look," said Jean, "the Umbralls and the Bonococcis. Shall we join them?"

"I don't know if I'm ready for Sylvia and Esther," Jim grunted.

"Too late," said Dorothy. "They've seen us."

They pushed two tables together and sat down with their friends. Sylvia was tall, slim, longish face, leggy and was compared to Eve Arden. Esther was shorter, five five, dark hair, round face. She was Brenda Vaccaro. Oscar was six six, 240 pounds, big fists, booming voice, the George Kennedy type. Finally, Carl was average, five eight, wiry, pleasant. A clown one minute then turned serious the next. He was compared to Burgess Meredith.

"What are you four guys up to?" Sylvia asked.

"We've been to Dr. Laura's office--and yes, before you ask," Dorothy looked at her two old friends and fellow teachers. "We found out that Jim and John were the two non-sterile survivors."

"Well, Jim," Oscar boomed. "You were always first in the class, you saved our mangy hides in the late disaster. Now maybe you can be the father of our community too."

"No thanks, Oscar," Dorothy replied for her husband. "Besides, what woman is there who can carry a child?"

"You can always import them," said Carl. "There's Asian Brides catalogs."

"We're still on our honeymoon and you're looking at Asian Brides magazine?" Sylvia scowled at him.

Carl turned to Oscar. "You're supposed to say: 'Surely you jest, Umbrall.' and then I say, 'I saw it at the doctor's office. It was five years old.'"

"Walter is the only doctor in town and Walter goes for nurses not Asian beauties. And if the magazine is five years old, those kids are already taken and have a dozen kids around the house," Sylvia glared at her husband.

"Please!" said Esther. "The subject of kids is strictly forbidden."

"Can we get to something serious here?" John cut in.

"If you want to talk serious, we'll have to move to another table," Jim glanced at Sylvia.

At that moment Jeff Randall came by and Jean and Dorothy invited him to sit at their table.

Jim saw that John was scowling. Something was bothering him. Apparently he had something on his mind and was trying to get it out. Instead he was frustrated by interruptions and attempts of humor.

While the others babbled away, Jim half turned his chair to face John. "We can discuss whatever you want in private if you wish. I don't know if anyone wants to take anything serious just now. You know, the sterility thing was a bad hit on everyone."

"I know, Jim. Jean took it hard, I'm sure. Although we haven't had a chance to talk since we left the doctor's office. And I can understand Sylvia's and Esther's eternal comedic routines. I like them. It helps get our minds off our problems. But something happened the other night that I think concerns everyone. It has to do with Martin, the cave and the 'children.'"

"And you want to discuss that with these jokesters sitting at this table? They'll make a joke of the whole thing when you're trying to be serious."

"Maybe that's what I need because I don't know if this is real or just a bad dream."

"All right, if that's what you want. They'll listen to you," he turned and pounded on the table until he got everyone's attention.

"John has something to tell us and I want everyone to pay attention and give him the courtesy of listening to his story. After that you're free to agree or disagree with what he said."

Everyone quieted down at Jim's announcement. Jim was still the most admired person in the class and in the community. He was the unofficial mayor of the city. And John, whose heritage had at one time elicited negative comments was now respected and accepted by the class. He had proven himself during the disaster of two years ago and was now considered like any member of the group.

"What I'm going to say, I know will elicit some humorous comments from Sylvia and Esther and disbelief from others. And ordinarily, I would have kept quiet because it would sound crazy or ridiculous. But it goes back to our experience two years ago. It left us with some unanswered questions--at least to Jim, Dorothy and me. That's why I decided to present this latest experience to get your views.

"Four nights ago I woke up, sometime after one in the morning. I don't know what woke me, maybe like anyone who wakes up during the night. Or maybe it was some unknown force that caused my awakening.

"I woke up staring at the ceiling. It was dark in the room yet not entirely so since some light came from the outside, enough to make out things in the room--the furniture, Jean sleeping next to me--and at the foot of the bed--those things."

"Oh, no!" Sylvia exclaimed.

John ignored her and continued. "Yes, what has been described by others as some form of humanoid. There were two of them, about the size of an eight or nine year old, pale bodies from what I could see--large black eyes, a small almost non-existent mouth.

"They didn't say or do anything, but just stared at me. I threw back the covers and got up. They didn't move. Standing there at the foot of the bed, they looked even smaller to me.

"That's when I heard the voice that I immediately recognized as Martin's, the old shaman of my tribe. 'John, John,' he said. 'It's Martin. Come to the cave. Bring the Children.'

"The voice was so clear like he was there in the room. I momentarily shifted my attention as if expecting to see Martin somewhere in the room. Then I saw the creatures had disappeared. There was no noise during all this time except for Martin's voice. And it didn't waken Jean.

"Later, I thought about it. I had been staring back at those things when Martin's voice broke in. It wasn't them because I couldn't see any perceptible movement of their mouths and there was no one else in the room. Was Martin's voice somehow transmitted into my senses through these creatures? That seemed to be the only reason for their appearance. They did nothing else I could see except stand at the foot of my bed. I checked the doors and windows and they were still locked from the inside. The ashes in the fireplace were undisturbed. No way that anyone could have come in and then out and not left some evidence of their presence.

"So, there it is. It disturbs me. It scares me."

"Surprise, surprise, John," Sylvia exclaimed. "I'm not going to belittle you. I happen to believe in flying saucers and UFO abductions."

"Somehow, it doesn't sound very supportive," said Oscar. "Sounded more like a sneak attack."

"O.K., let's not get started on that," said Jim. "I know John is serious and he wouldn't be subjecting himself to ridicule for the hell of it. So, let's discuss this in a rational and intelligent manner, no matter what your personal feelings or beliefs are."

"Why didn't you wake me up," Jean asked. "Then you would have had a witness,"

"Because it happened so fast and it was so unbelievable. I just didn't think. Later it was too late."

"I'm hurt you didn't confide in me and that I have to learn about it this way," Jean was grim.

"I'm sorry. All along I wondered if it was just a dream. I've never seen a UFO or had any other supernatural experience. Then suddenly it's there. Now I'm questioning my sanity."

Dorothy gripped Jean's arm. "Don't be too hard on him. Men do these sort of things without thinking. It doesn't mean they think less of you for doing it."

"Dorothy's right," said Jim. "I've screwed up royally with her, but I wouldn't trade her for ten of Hollywood's beauty queens."

"How about eleven?" Sylvia had to ask.

"See what I put up with from my so-called friends," Dorothy grinned.

"Aw, now my feelings are hurt," Sylvia smacked her forehead.

"You kids are getting out of control again," Jim stopped the by-play. "Let's get back and examine John's problem."

"Let's assumed everything is legitimate," said Carl. "What do you make of it? What do you think it means?"

"I believe everyone here has been told of what happened before the catastrophe," John looked around the table, "except for Jeff. So let me do a quick review.

"There was this cave on our reservation that was held to be sacred to the tribe. No one was allowed access to it except the chief and the tribal medicine man, Martin. He expressed quite an interest in me at an early age, even wanted to make me his heir in the medicine business. But I wasn't ready at the time. Nevertheless, he took me to the cave and showed me around. There was this stack of old tablets with inscriptions on them which I couldn't make out. Neither did Martin. He said they had been in the cave since he first entered it and according to his predecessors, even before then.

"Martin also told me about the legends of our people. One was the story of the First Children who survived when the last world ended. They survived to repopulate the new world. But it was also foretold that even this new world would end. A new group would survive to jumpstart the next new world. They were the Chosen Ones or First Children. The identity of these new survivors would be revealed to the last shaman of the tribe. Martin told me he had identified me as one by means I do not know or can vouch for. Apparently he saw an aura and upon touching a person, he would know this person was one of the children. But Martin never found any more, though he searched throughout the reservation.

"Then, still curious about the tablets in the cave, I persuaded Martin I knew an archaeologist we could trust to keep the cave a secret. This is where Jim came in. As soon as Martin saw him, he almost jumped out of his skin. Jim was one of us, he said. Jim and I scoffed at the idea. Jim couldn't believe a white man had a role in an Indian legend. But he went along with Martin because of his interest in the tablets. And as soon as he saw the tablets, everything else was forgotten. Jim was in his element. But Martin wanted to maintain secrecy so he wouldn't let Jim bring in a team of scientists. Martin said Jim and I could do it alone. Jim had no choice but to accept.

"Meantime, Martin's meeting with Jim and his disclosure that Jim was part of the legend, opened new possibilities for Martin. Jim and I came from Stonecliff and went to school together, was it possible there was a connection?

"Jim needed supplies and equipment for the tablet project, so we went to Stonecliff. Martin insisted on going along, intrigued by the possibilities there might be more 'children' there.

"Martin came along with me when I visited Thelma Rattling, the only one with whom I had corresponded. Jim went to the Post to order supplies and there met Dorothy again. The start of a beautiful romance."

Jim and Dorothy clasped hands in remembrance. "The most important and beautiful day of my life," Dorothy beamed. Jim kissed her.

"Oh, mush!" Sylvia exclaimed, but she also had a smile on her face.

"Yes," John continued. "A most important day, for Martin claimed Thelma was one of the children. Then later, upon meeting Dorothy, she was also added to the list. After that, there was no stopping him from thinking the rest of his children were residing in Stonecliff. The evidence seemed overwhelming. All four of the known ones had grown up in the same city and gone to school together. So Martin pestered Dorothy about meeting more of her classmates, that's why Dorothy finally agreed to hold that high school reunion and inviting Martin so he could see the rest of the class."

"Aha!" Sylvia yelped. "I knew there was something behind that reunion."

"Oh, shut up, Syl," Dorothy shushed her. "Let John finish."

"So the reunion was set and Martin was supposed to be there on Wednesday," John took up the story again. "In the meantime Martin speeded up the stocking of the cave which he claimed would shelter and save the survivors. The rest you know. The reunion never made it past that Monday."

Everyone had been absorbed with the story that the food lay uneaten. Even those who knew it or had heard it were no less impressed with the retelling.

It was Jeff Randall who broke the silence. "I know I'm a stranger here and I may be viewed as an intruder in a family matter, but I was intrigued by all you said. I would like to see the cave if it is permitted by the tribe. I'm a spelunker, although cavers don't like that term. And the more scientifically inclined, term themselves as speleologists. So if you are contemplating a journey there, I would like to offer what little expertise I have in that field."

"Well, thank you, Jeff. You've just about helped me make a decision. I'm going there. You want to come along, Jeff, you're welcome."

"John, are you sure this is necessary?" Jim told him. "We believe you. No one will think less of you if you pass it off as an anomaly."

"I have to, Jim. We never did find out for sure what happened to Martin. Maybe he's back there, needing our help. I have to know."

"But after two years, dear," Jean held his arm.

"It could be amnesia," said Sylvia.

"Of course, amnesia, the ultimate soap opera cliche," said Esther, "along with the eternal triangle and the resurrection of long dead actors."

Jim grimaced at the jokesters. "All right, go there to ease your mind. In fact, I'll go along with you. An archaeologist contributes zero to building a new town. Besides, I'm still mystified as to what happened to those tablets."

"Damn!" Dorothy exclaimed. "There you go, taking off again. You know what happened the last time you did that."

"Darling, you have a business to set up and I'm no help in that area. It's plain nepotism to keep me on the payroll."

"You want to get away, don't you? Are you tired of domestic life?"

"I never shall," he took her in his arms.

"Very well. If you go, than I do too."

"But what about the store?"

"I have competent help who can carry on for me."

"If Dorothy goes, so do I," said Jean.

"Why don't we all go?" Carl looked at Oscar for confirmation. "We can make it an outing. A weekend for picnics and riding and a visit to a cavern."

"I don't mind," said Oscar. "It might pay for me to check that area for the Forest Service to see if any vegetation is coming up after the disaster. Of course, it's reservation land and there might be objections."

"Not from me, Oscar," John told him. "I guess I'm the highest ranking official left from the tribe."

"Movie title!" shrieked Esther.

"The Last of the Mohicans," Sylvia retorted.

Everyone laughed. John rolled his eyes.

CHAPTER FIVE

The reservation belonging to John's tribe was to the southeast of Stonecliff. It had fared no better than the rest of the devastated area. It was empty of human habitation. A few of the tribesmen had survived by having left the reservation. In the last two years, John had been in touch with them, urging them to return to the land of their ancestors. So far none had been willing. This had played havoc with John's plans to rebuild the reservation to what it had been before the catastrophe--cattle ranches, skiing and fishing resorts.

John, with Jim and Aaron's help, had managed to have a gravel road cleared through the notch in the mountain chain. It was barely wide enough for two vehicles, but it did provide for swifter transportation than to depend on horses.

They picked the July 4th holiday for their outing. Two vans would carry the ten people, five couples. The four women, Dorothy, Jean, Sylvia and Esther had conspired to lure Dr. Laura on the trip. They had done this by dangling the prospect of researching an area the survivors had visited, particularly Jim and John. It didn't matter that aside from those two, only eight others had gone into the area and only for a limited amount of time. And a woman of Laura's intelligence must have realized that. But whether she did or not, she succumbed to the entreaties of the four women. Perhaps she was lonely, combined with the holiday weekend that decided her. They did not tell her Jeff was also going. Nor was he aware she was on the other van, since they were picked up separately.

They had supplied themselves appropriately. Food and drink mostly although John had told them there was water aplenty and the food stored by Martin was probably still good, especially in the cool temperatures of the cave.

Jeff had advised them on the proper equipment for cave exploring. They had brought along heavy duty clothes which they could change into if they went deep into the cavern. Most were wearing shorts and light clothing because of the season. Jeff also brought harnesses, nylon rope, flashlights, matches, blankets and mountaineering equipment. John told him some of those supplies were already in the cave since Martin had tried to foresee all possible situations.

Ever careful, Jim made sure someone knew where they were going, so he informed the Sherlands, Granhills and the Wadleys. Tom was somewhat put out for not being invited. Jim encouraged him and anyone else who so desired to join them at the cave and gave him directions.

John also brought along some other equipment that drew puzzled exclamations--firearms.

"Guns! Why do we need those for?" Dr. Laura was the most vehement.

"It pays to be prepared. Haven't you ever heard of the Boy Scouts?" John answered. He had brought along two rifles and three revolvers.

"We're going by past experience," said Jim. "Two years ago, just one revolver in the hands of the wrong person caused a lot of misery and havoc."

"Amen to that--and pass the ammunition," added Oscar.

"Martin probably stored some firearms in the cave," continued Jim. "Two years ago, at least eighteen people died or were missing, two wounded. Out of these twenty casualties, eleven were by gunfire or explosives. Twelve bodies have never been found. I'm sure they're out there under the rubble and debris--maybe someday..."

The two vans met at the edge of town and at this time, Laura discovered the identity of the last passenger.

"What is he doing here? Did he know I was coming?" she glared suspiciously at Dorothy.

"Oh, yeah, we needed an extra couple that could keep us entertained with their constant bickering," Dorothy quipped.

"Come on, Jeff was there when we planned the trip. He asked to come along. Said he was an amateur caver and could help us if we were to explore the cave.

"You were asked to come along because the cave and the Indian superstitions played a part in our recent ordeal. And of course we consider you our friend as much as we feel the same towards Jeff. Should we have to make a choice between friends?

"Forgive me if I get a little judgmental. But as a bystander and observer, it seems the enmity is more from your side. I think you do Jeff an injustice and I'm sure he's just as puzzled at your attitude as we are. However, I respect your right to choose your friends and companions. Stay away from him as well as you can. I'm sure he'll get the idea that he's not wanted."

Grim-faced, Laura tossed her bag inside the van and climbed in with Dorothy and Jean who shared the back seat. John was driving with Jim next to him. Jeff was in the second van with the Umbralls and the Bonococcis.

It was an eighty mile ride that would take about two hours the vans had four-wheel drive because the last few miles to the cave would be over terrain without roads. John had been unwilling to lay a road to the cave entrance, doubtless, Jim thought, as one last concession to Martin's obsession for secrecy.

Laura, still smarting from Dorothy's comments, was

silent at the beginning of the trip. Hoping to raise her spirits Jean and Dorothy told her their stories of their romance with their husbands.

The Mexican-American girl and the half Indian boy gravitated to a group made up of other outsiders. They all lived in the River Road area, inhabited by the poor, the minorities and other social outcasts deemed inferior through reason of birth, race or social position. And even within that neighborhood, bigotry existed.

Jean had encouraged John to rise above the hatred and intolerance and with her help he did. That is until their graduation when he professed his love for her and she pushed him away. Her family would not accept him and she was expected to marry within her own ethnic group. So bigotry reared its ugly head and Jean was unable to go against her family's wishes.

John went back to the reservation refusing to go to college which the tribe had been prepared to subsidize. He spent a miserable year working on a ranch, feeling sorry for himself. His misery was compounded when he learned she had married a suitable Mexican-American boy.

Eventually he went to college and returned to help run the various business interests of the tribe. He rarely went to Stonecliff, He never saw Jean again until the reunion.

"I was an insufferable, naive fool," said Jean. "All those schoolgirl ideals. If only real life lived up to those ideals. Fortunately, I was given a second chance--but at what costs."

"Your decision at an early age didn't lead to a disaster in order to rectify it," Laura told her. "You didn't buy your happiness in exchange for those thousands who lost their lives in Stonecliff."

"I know it," replied Jean, misty eyed. "Nevertheless, I've felt guilt at my happiest moments."

John, driving, extended his hand back. She grasped it like a drowning person grasping a lifeline.

"Of course it doesn't make sense," said Laura. "Don't you know that? You're a woman. Women are not supposed to be logical. We're allowed to cry for the simplest of reasons."

She took Jean's other hand.

The others were very quiet, the only sound was from the gravel hurled by centrifugal force from the tires and striking the tire wells.

"It was different with Jim and me," Dorothy broke the silence. "We weren't high school sweethearts or even had one date. His love interest was Linda Bonner, later Storey and now Sherland. She was the Grace Kelley of Stonecliff High."

Jim, half turned in the front seat, smiled. "She doesn't let me forget.

"It wasn't that I didn't notice her. We were both class officers. She was, is, a very intelligent woman, smarter than me. She was also an enigma. I saw her on the sidelines at a football game, leading the cheers--a beautiful, shapely cheerleader. Then the next day in class, in the halls, there she was apparently uncaring or careless in her appearance."

"Jim's right about that last part," Dorothy nodded. "I think now, it was a reaction to Linda. She was always prim and proper, dressed very day as if she was attending a social. So, maybe, I subconsciously rebelled and did the opposite. So I got involved in every school project that I got a reputation as a leader of new or lost causes."

"We didn't see each other again until two years ago," Jim took up the story. "I was in her father's store when she came up behind me and spoke to the clerk. When I turned around I was stunned by the beautiful woman I saw. It took a few minutes before we realized who each other was. I was much taken by her and for a while I forgot her name was now Walters, not Perkins, and a very married lady."

"Yes, thinking back now," Dorothy looked out the car window, "I was delighted to meet Jim again. We saw each other quite often after that, especially after we were linked by Martin as being part of his 'children' legend. I made several trips to the reservation that summer to watch the work on the tablets Jim was working on. I guess I started getting too interested and made a trip too many. Jim brought me up short. It was quite embarrassing. I swore never to go back. I was a married woman although at the time I didn't know but suspected my husband was philandering. So, I didn't see Jim again until the reunion, eight months later."

"I wish I had known," Jim broke in, "about your husband. I would have acted differently--then again I didn't know how you felt."

"I didn't know either," she said. "But then came the day of the reunion. A momentous day it was and in a way no one would suspect. The world would change for all time for all of us. Like Jean said, we finally achieved happiness but at a great cost to our families. But I can live with that now because it was nothing I did to cause it."

"Let me finish the story for Laura," said Jim. "When John and I got to the reunion, Sylvia, as usual, took to making cracks about everyone, some not too flattering. Included was one directed to Linda and me that referred to old romances. This angered Linda so that she felt, I suspect, she had to draw attention away from us. So, she openly flirted with Tom Wadley, well known as an NFL quarterback. She proposed that he, Tom, escort her around the reunion activities. Since Oscar and Esther had some catching up to do, that left Dorothy and me together and I took full advantage of that.

"There's not much left after that. The disaster came. It seemed to fit Martin's legend of impending disaster that John, Dorothy and myself came to believe it was the end of one world and the start of another. When we came out of the shelter, we saw what had happened to the town. There were no survivors. And as time went on and no one came to rescue us, we came to realized there were no ties to bind us to that old world. I declared my love for her and she accepted."

"There was a postscript to that," Dorothy interjected. "My husband did survive with one of those survivalist groups. One member of his group found me running away from Larry Wilk, who had kidnapped me. This man took me to his group and there I found my ex-husband with his girlfriend. Imagine the surprise for both of us. Meanwhile Jim and John had trailed me and rescued me after my husband abandoned me to one of his cohorts. Later that group came after us and attacked us. My husband was killed when Martin blew up the mountain. This very one we're traveling now."

"And we've lived happily ever after," Jim finished.

Laura was entranced with the romantic tales she had heard. She had forgotten her irritation over having Jeff along on the trip.

"Ah," she said. "It's like reading a romance novel. And that's where I've gotten all my romance lately, from a book."

Dorothy looked at Jean and winked. Laura's comment was a straight line aching to be answered.

"Romance is everywhere and all around you," Dorothy replied. "You just have to recognize it."

"Oh great! What an answer," Jim snorted. "Did I miss that? Was that on a Berma Shave sign on the road?

"Romance or love, call it what you will, comes down to two things: 'man--woman.' Whichever one you are, you need the other. It's binomial."

"The archaeologist speaks," Dorothy sniffed. "After several millenniums of history and artifacts unearthed from its debris, he narrows it down to binomial--man, woman. When hasn't it been otherwise?"

Jean turned to Laura. "Sounds like these two have spent too much time with Sylvia and Esther. They have their routines down pat."

Everyone laughed. Laura was in a good mood as John turned off the road and headed for the cave.

CHAPTER SIX

Since the disaster, access to the devastated area had been limited. That didn't mean that some adventuresome types hadn't tried and some had probably succeeded without the authorities being any wiser. For that reason, John had camouflaged the entrance to the cave. Prior to the catastrophe, natural vegetation had accomplished that. Even so, he was still worried that someone would eventually stumble into the entrance.

For some time now, he had entreated the government to help clear up the reservation. But the government was reluctant to spend more money since there was only one survivor on the reservation. For that reason he had tried to get some members of the tribe to return. Most of them had migrated to California, a few to Tucson and Las Vegas. Only two families had expressed interest, but even this response had not been very enthusiastic.

The two vans pulled up a few yards from the entrance. They too would be camouflaged with netting John had brought in previous trips. The vans were unloaded and the supplies and equipment carried to the entrance of the cave.

"How many people know about this?" Jeff asked.

"Present company excluded, the Wadleys, the Jabotys and the Kendalls and Aaron Sherland. Aaron has been here recently, helping to open the road. The others were here shortly after the disaster, but not since," replied John.

"But if this is a sacred place, why are you showing it to me and Mr. Randall?" Laura asked. Jeff winced at the 'mister.'

"These are all my friends--like family. Perhaps like I told you in the story earlier today, they are more than that. As for you and Jeff, I consider you my friends as well. If that isn't enough, just consider this a special dispensation on my part," he winked at her.

"Pope John!" Sylvia exclaimed.

"Don't be blasphemous," Esther ordered.

"You know," Sylvia peered into the dark innards of the cave, "the last time I went underground, an awful thing happened."

"It couldn't have been that awful," grinned Oscar. "You're still here."

"The awful thing is that we're going to be without our TV sets," said Esther.

"Not to worry," said Carl. "I think I brought a TV Guide with me."

"Sadist!" shouted Sylvia.

Only Jeff and Laura paid any attention to this byplay.

"It does raise a question," said Jim. "Do we camp outside the entrance or inside, say by the pool?"

"A pool?" Laura raised an eyebrow.

"We spared no cost," Dorothy replied, "although it may be a bit cool for you."

"A cool pool," laughed Sylvia.

"Why don't we just leave our stuff here by the entrance," said Jim. "Then we'll explore a ways and see how everyone feels. Hopefully no one is claustrophobic."

"You had to mention that word," complained Sylvia.

"Just imagine yourself back in the Dungeon," Dorothy smiled sweetly. That being Sylvia's nickname for the school basement where they were trapped during the disaster

"Another sadist," Sylvia stuck her tongue out at Dorothy.

"It's close to the noon hour," said John. "Why don't we eat, then start a tour after that?" To which everyone was agreeable

After lunch John lighted some lanterns and led them into the cave. A hundred yards in, they began to encounter boxes and crates lined by the walls. Alcoves were full

All were part of the supplies brought in by Martin. Finally, they entered a level of the cave that resembled a balcony. Down below they could see a large pool of water. Light reflected from the pool as John held a lantern aloft.

"Oh, gorgeous," said Laura. "Like another world."

"It is another world," Jeff answered her, "quiet, cool and spectacular. The nearest thing to the dawn of time, without the dawn, of course. If you crave solitude or the time to examine your life, this is it. Yet for some, it is scary and not for those who can't stand loneliness."

"Next you'll be telling us it's the return to the womb," cracked Sylvia.

"That was an unkind remark," Laura admonished her.

"Thank you," said Jeff. "I wasn't trying to put on some pretense of knowledge or disclose some profound truth. I grew up in Kentucky which has so many caves that it must be hollow underneath.

"I remember when I was ten or eleven, I ran away and hid in one such cave. Happily for me, it wasn't one with a vertical entrance or my bones would still be there.

"I sat there thinking how sorry my family and friends would feel when they found me gone. There! That would teach them. I explored the cave as far as I could. I had brought candles for that purpose since I had decided to hide there, beforehand. I was excited by the beauty of the rock formations yet fearful of what the darkness might hide. My imagination was in overdrive and I had visions of weird creatures lurking just beyond the flickering shadows produced by the light from my candle. My fears got the best of me and I fled back to the entrance. There I stayed until dark. The light from my candles stood out in the dark and that's how they found me."

"And you got properly punished," said Esther.

"Yes, but first they hugged and kissed me before they got serious and meted out the punishment."

"Apparently it didn't cure you of dark holes in the ground," observed Laura.

Dorothy and Jean exchanged glances as they noted Laura's conciliatory tone.

"No, because I found it a form of peace and relaxation to spend time in a place like this. Sometimes when I have a problem, I find the solitude conducive to solving it."

"And what problem is burdening your mind now?" Laura persisted.

"Problem? I came along because of my interests in caves. But problems I always have. It's always a matter of degree. Like frustrations in your job, puzzlement in personal relationships. Don't you find that to be true?"

"Uh--yes, at times."

Dorothy nudged Jean with her elbow.

The interlude was broken up, as usual, by Sylvia. "Hey! I got problems. Does anyone want to hear about..."

"No!" almost in unison.

It was cool and the women were wearing shorts, so they decide to return to the entrance.

"Wait!" cried Sylvia. "There! Did you see it?"

"What?" Carl was next to her.

"I saw something move out there."

"What was it?"

"I don't know. It was so fast. Like a flash out of the corner of your eye." Oscar laughed. "Our lady of wit is scared witless. Jeff's tale of fearful creatures has got her imagination running."

"You could have seen something," said Jeff. "There are creatures in these caverns. But not the kind out of a Hollywood horror film. Not likely they'll come near you if they can help it. Some are either blind or have developed their eyesight to exist in the dark down here. Their whole body structure might have changed millenniums ago to reflect their changed environment."

They were returning to the entrance as they talked. Sylvia had forged to the front, but still cast anxious glances to the rear of their column.

"How would these creatures look?" from Carl, ever the inquisitive scientist even though he was only a high school science teacher.

"Probably from the reptile family. I leave them alone and they return the favor. I'm not into the study of the cave inhabitants, only the caves and their formations."

"That does it!" said Sylvia. "Carl, we're out of here!"

"Don't be a spoilsport," said Jeff. "With the light and noise we generate, they'll be out of here too."

"That's an interesting comment about changing their bodies," Carl mused aloud, still mulling Jeff's earlier comment and ignoring Sylvia's lament.

"Every creature adapts to its environment in order to survive," said Jim. "Not all make it, but what emerges is the hardier for it. That's what keeps me in business.

"It wasn't too long ago we were all in the same shape. No buttons to push, no phone, or radio, or TV, no set of wheels to take us where we wanted. We had become slaves of modern society with its trappings of convenience."

"But we did function," said Carl.

"Yes, but for how long? We were lucky. We existed for several months. What we made do with, much would have been used up or deteriorated eventually. You can check these supplies Martin hoarded. How good are they still? What if our situation had become permanent?"

"An end to our world is not something we'll likely see in our lifetime," said Jeff. "Only self-proclaimed prophets like to push that line for their own personal interests. Meanwhile life will go on. War followed by peace, peace followed by war. Winter followed by spring, then by summer and fall. Then we begin the cycle again."

"That's the old uniformitarianism versus catastrophism argument," said Carl. "Or put in terms Sylvia can understand, your everyday humdrum life goes on and on without change like Jeff said. Others maintain that there have been constant changes in the past and they shall continue into the present and future. It was the latter that worried us during our recent calamity."

"Catastrophes happen all the time," said Jim. "Earthquakes, hurricanes, floods, volcanic eruptions, it is really a matter of degree and scope. You might say we have uniformitarianism occasionally interrupted by catastrophism.

"That is to say, to quote Carl, your plain everyday humdrum life is suddenly beset by an incident that causes a big change, in an individual, a country or the whole planet. After the interruption, uniformitarianism may resume for another long period although along a different path and under different circumstances until another interruption occurs and we start the cycle again."

"Oh great! Now we've got three double-domes spouting scientific mumbo-jumbo," Sylvia turned to Dorothy. "You may never see your husband again. He and Carl and Jeff are lost in space."

"From the TV series of the same name," said Esther.

"Well, if he prefers their company to mine," Dorothy lifted the hem of her skirt, exposing her gorgeous leg. "What can a poor girl like me do?"

"Yeah, yeah, you're a big help," Sylvia turned away in disgust. "The old seduction bit. You just turned the feminist movement back a hundred years."

"Well," said Oscar, "the way Jim said it makes sense to me, but then, who am I to say anything. I made a D in science. And that's why I ended up playing football and nursing trees for the Forest Service."

"Okay, big boy," Sylvia had to have her say. "When you got tackled and crashed to the ground that was science, otherwise called gravity. The aftereffects of the crash on the ground generates an earthquake which is measured and called seismology. That's a form of science too."

"How do you 'splain nursin' trees?" Esther asked in her best Ricky Ricardo accent.

"That's a tough one, Ricky, but I guess keeping dogs from raising their hind legs must qualify for something in the line of duty."

"I've got some science for you, Sylvia," Oscar glared at her. "Pow! Straight to the moon. Some people call that rocket science."

"Ralph Kramden to Alice in the 'Honeymooners,'" said Esther.

"Does this go on all the time?" Laura asked.

"For longer than you can imagine," Dorothy smiled.

They finished out the day by the entrance, only John venturing any distance back into the cave. They ate that evening around a campfire.

"We can sleep in our sleeping bags just inside the entrance or outside as you please. The weather will get cool, probably down to the 50s," Jim told them, "but otherwise there should be no problems. We can keep the fire going. Whoever gets up during the night can replenish it."

"Not me," exclaimed Sylvia. "Come on, Carl, we're sleeping in the van."

"Great," said Oscar. "I'd rather Carl be the one kept up all night with her yakking."

"Gee, I used to sleep-walk," replied Sylvia. "I might just visit you tonight."

"You do that, but be careful you don't step on any snakes."

"Snakes?"

"Yeah, you know, those long, wiggling, slimy..."

"Come on, Carl," Sylvia pulled him up. "It's our time to guard the van."

"Yeah, right," Oscar looked at Esther and winked.

So the Umbralls went to the van. The others found their spot around the fire, Laura between Dorothy and Jean, their husbands on the other side. The Bonococcis and Jeff completed the circle.

The campfire blazed throwing light around a circle that included the bundled forms. Jim and Dorothy had a large sleeping bag that accommodated two and the others must have heard the giggles coming from it. But since no one could see faces or read thoughts, no one knew the reactions of the others.

With time the circle of light became smaller as the fire used up its fuel. The sleeping forms became motionless.

Then came the scream in the night.

CHAPTER SEVEN

There was enough room in the rear of the van with the rear seat pushed forward for two people to lie down, full length and side by side. Carl and Sylvia made themselves comfortable, or as comfortable as one can get on the hard bed of a van with only a sleeping bag to cushion their bodies.

"No way was I going to sleep out there--not with snakes about," she shuddered.

"Uh-huh," Carl, automatically replied, his mind still trying to find that elusive thought that kept eluding him in his earlier discussion with Jim and Jeff.

"Yeah, I know, Oscar was trying to scare me--the big oaf thinks he did."

"Yes--well, there are probably some out there," Carl temporarily roused himself to answer her. "Insects and reptiles are the most likely species to have survived our recent calamity. They could hide in any little hole or crevasse measuring a fraction of an inch.

"Remember 'The Incredible Shrinking Man?'" figuring that was the best way to make his point with his movie struck wife.

"Yeah, but if they're small, they could just as well have been blown away with those terrible winds."

"Some, but not all. Most wild life can sense or have a premonition of an impending change in their environment."

"How did we stray into this subject?"

"As I recall, my dear, you brought it up. Snakes? Remember?

"Oscar won the battle," he grinned. "He got you rattled with the snakes-everywhere-you-step bit." Carl turned over trying to get his thoughts back on his problem.

"That's what he thinks," Sylvia snarled. "I've got plans for that big jock."

She looked out the rear windows which faced the sleeping campers. But the windows were only half the length of the door and from her position, she couldn't see her friends, only the flickering glow of the fire.

So she stared at the window, planning her revenge on Oscar. The two had carried on their feud for the last two years when Oscar had returned to Stonecliff for the reunion. He had eventually reunited with his ex-wife, Esther and Sylvia's close friend. To anyone outside the group, their bickering and barbed comments would have provoked anyone else to call 911. Actually they were very good friends with high regard for each other. And the whole group knew that, which was why no one got too excited when they went after each other with their war of words.

So as she looked out, her mind had not entirely rid its thoughts of snakes. She hated them. How many little holes and crevasses were there in a van? She shifted uncomfortably. Weren't they supposed to seek warmth and heat--maybe under her sleeping bag?

She sat up abruptly, gingerly looking about her. In vain, of course. It was too dark inside the van to see much. Damn it! Carl was right. Oscar had gotten to her. He was probably snickering in his sleeping bag now.

She ought to go out there and repay him. But how? Out of the corner of her eye there was a flicker of movement. She turned. On the window, a face was pressed against the glass, peering in. She screamed!

The face disappeared.

Carl came upright. "What!"

Oscar! She thought. It's got to be him. She got up and opened the door." Come on. I'm going to get that trickster." She jumped to the ground and went striding towards the campers, fifty feet away. They too, were sitting up.

Jim and Dorothy untangled themselves from their gab and stood as Sylvia reached them, Carl trailing behind her.

"Was that you?" Jim asked.

"Damn right! Some peeping Tom was sneaking a peek into our van. And I know who it was," she headed for Oscar who was sitting up and with open palm smacked him on his head.

"Hey! What was that for?" Oscar felt his head.

"You know damn well what it's for. You weren't satisfied with the snake stories, you had to go rattle my cage. That slap is just the beginning, there's more to come. Oh boy, revenge is going to be sweet."

"Are you saying Oscar was peeping into the van to scare you?" Jim was disbelieving.

"Hello? Excuse me? Didn't I make myself clear?"

"But it couldn't have been Oscar, Sylvia," Esther spoke up. "I heard the scream--your scream. It couldn't have been more than a few seconds that I heard it. Oscar was right here, next to me. He couldn't have run back and get in the sack in that short a time."

"I concur," said Laura. "I'm a light sleeper. As soon as I heard the scream, I woke up and lifted my head. There was no running in this direction or even standing up. It was no one from this group that was around the fire."

Sylvia looked from one woman to the other. One was her best friend and longtime companion in their bachelor days, the other a respected doctor with a professional mind and no axes to grind.

"Well--who else could it have been? Oscar's the only one who would play a trick on me."

"Maybe it wasn't a trick." said Dorothy.

"It wasn't one of our bunch," said John. "He didn't, wouldn't come this way. He would run away when you screamed and he would run away from the camp. He had to have seen the fire and the bunch of us sleeping around it.

"In the morning I'll check the area around the van. He probably left a trail in the brush that will be easy to follow. It's too dark now to do anything and we would probably mess up any evidence out there."

"John's right," Jim nodded. "But we'll set up a guard until morning, two hour shifts should..."

"I'll take the first two," said Jeff.

"Okay, wake me up in two hours," said Jim. "That should get us to midnight, then Oscar, Carl and John."

"How about the women?" Sylvia asked.

"No guard duty for the ladies," said Jim. "But I have no objections if a lady wants to join the guard on duty."

"Where are you going to sleep, Sylvia?" Carl asked her.

"Well, not back in the van."

"It's not likely he'll return," said Jim. "He knows there's too many of us."

"I'll take my chances here," she said.

"You can sleep next to me," said Oscar. "That way you can keep an eye on me."

"Oh, I'll be keeping an eye on you. You won't know when or where I'm going to strike. You'll need eyes on the back of your thick skull."

"I'm shaking already," he grinned, "thinking to wake up in the middle of the night, your head inches away from mine.

"Guys," he looked at the others. "The next scream you hear will be mine."

"Har-de-har-har," Sylvia snarled.

"You shouldn't have screamed right away," Oscar continued. "You should have put your own face to the glass and scared him away without screaming. Or maybe he would have been the one to scream. As it is now, we don't have any identification of the intruder. For all we know, it was the 'Creature from the Black Lagoon.'

"Was he hairless, slimy and with big, black bulging eyes?"

Sylvia eyed him. "Oh, you're going to get it. I promise you. If there's a God in heaven, I'm..."

Carl snapped his fingers. "That's it!"

"What now?" from Jim.

"What you and I and Jeff were talking about earlier. How species change in order to adapt to its new environment.

"When Oscar mentioned hairless, slimy, bulging eyed creatures, it rang a bell. Doesn't that sound like the creatures John described as visiting his home?

"Just think about it. They're short, hairless and with big eyes. Doesn't that describe the perfect cave creature? Short, perfect for the small spaces in a cave. Grayish, hairless skin, you don't get any color inside a dark cave. Overly large eyes--think of taking a picture, the darker it is, the larger the diameter of your lens. In bright sunlight, the aperture of your lens is down to a pinpoint. A creature with these characteristics would never walk the surface of this planet--except at night. During daylight hours, it could only exist in a dark place--or a cave.

"John's description of his visitors tally with descriptions given by others claiming abductions or encounters with similar beings."

"And you're deducing, what?" John asked.

"These creatures came to you. You heard a voice telling you to come to this cave. These creatures fit a description that fits a denizen of the underworld of caverns.

"Those who have seen them, label them as aliens from some far-off planet inhabited by people with a higher civilization when in fact, they may be home-grown, living in a labyrinth under our feet, or simply, in a cave."

"I can't believe this," exclaimed Sylvia. "In the middle of the night, isolated in a wilderness and my husband is talking scientific theory."

"Sorry, Syl. It's been bothering all day and it just came together when Oscar made that crack. Great discoveries aren't always made under the best of conditions."

"I'll tell that to Mr. Nobel when you get your award."

"That's a very interesting theory, Carl," said Jim. "But it's late. I think everyone has had a long day. Let's get our sleep."

"I don't think I'll be able to sleep now," said Carl.

Sylvia threw up her hands and plopped down next to Esther while Carl went for the sleeping bags.

"Great! He gets excited over some theory and can't sleep. I can't sleep because I keep seeing snakes and faces in the window."

She thought she heard suppressed laughter from Oscar's sleeping bag. She took off her shoe and threw it at his bag.

CHAPTER EIGHT

Jeff took his watch sitting by the cave entrance, a Winchester across his lap. It was just as well he wasn't trying to sleep. He could see the forms around the campfire as they tried to regain their sleep.

As for himself, he used this time to ponder Carl's startling theory. He was one of many who took an avid interest in the paranormal although he didn't consider himself a fanatic on the subject. He didn't belong to any organization that believed in such things. Nor did he attend any seminars or conventions on the subject. Yet he considered himself an independent observer of the phenomena. And, of course, a man in his position couldn't be too public on such matters without it rubbing off on his employer, the congressman. The tabloids would have a field day.

At that instance he saw one of the campers sit up. For a few seconds the sleeper, or non-sleeper as it seemed, remained in the sitting position. Then he arose--no, it was a she as he saw the long hair. The woman turned, saw him then after a moment's hesitation, walked towards him. It was

Laura.

"Trouble sleeping?" he asked as she got close.

"Isn't everyone?" she countered.

He shrugged, mentally irked by her combativeness. "I see they're in a prone position, so I assume they're trying or have succeeded. But who knows what goes on in the privacy of one's sleeping bag."

"Spoken like a lawyer," she laughed.

"I notice that seems to bother you."

"Don't have much use for them."

"I know how you meant that. But realistically, they're everywhere. You buy a house, a car, anything that requires a contract and there they are. Our laws, rules and regulations are made up by them. I am aware of the low esteem in which they are held."

"Then why are you one of them?"

"It's a living. But presently it's mostly PR, a change from my previous employment. It was a family thing, you know, like father like son."

"You find doing PR for a congressman more challenging than what you did before? What a dog of a job you must have had."

"Yes it was. As for the present job, look where I've been these past few months. Look where I am now, with a rifle across my knees."

He resisted taking a jab at her own situation. He was tired of retaliation every time he made any statement.

She nodded and sat down. "Your description could very well be mine.

"Look, I'm sorry about taking off on you. My experience with politics hasn't been very pleasant. Somehow it always seems to have priority over medicine. It's comparable to health administrators worried more about the cost factors while ignoring the healing and care that medicine is all about. More and more that process is given secondary status."

"I agree. And I can understand that because it's true in almost any organization you can think of. It is sickening that it is also found in charitable and religious groups. The do'ers are at the bottom while those on top carve out empires to fatten their wallets."

"Ah, a radical lawyer, a bleeding-heart liberal.

"So, you're planning to do what?"

"I might just stay out here and help do some empire building with these people. Just look around you. How much needs to be done."

She shook her head. "Poor guys. They'll have no children to help them."

"None of their own perhaps. But there's always adoption and I heard them mention fertility drugs."

"Adoption is possible. As for the drugs, it depends on whether their condition would be helped by them. Then too, we have to find if their sterility is permanent. It could be temporary. We may never know what brought it about."

"I like them. For their sake I hope there's an answer."

"I'm not trying to change the subject, but what do you think of all this," she asked.

"Which 'this' are you referring to? Sylvia's encounter a while ago or Carl's theory relating to what John saw in his house?"

"Well, I was thinking of Sylvia. The other thing sounds so preposterous."

"Then there's a lot of people out there with preposterous stories. The number of people who have had some sort of supernatural encounters must now number in the millions. They can't all be kooks or nuts. Indeed, some are well respected professionals--including doctors."

"All right, that's one for you," she held up her forefinger and checked off an invisible tally in the air. "It doesn't mean it happened here. There's only one person's word."

"As a doctor and as one who has dealt with John and his wife, does he strike you as one to make such a claim and do it publicly?"

"No. From all I know, he's very practical and honest. Not the type to seek publicity. Everyone here, from the class, likes and admires him."

"I agree with everything you just said. So what's your

problem?"

"Oh, you can be so infuriating," she started to get up, but he grasped her hand and held her back.

"Look, I want to be friends and if we're going to be, you have to understand something. That every time I say or do something that contradicts your views, it doesn't mean I dislike you or want to take over because of some macho mentality. Friends can have differing opinions, but it doesn't mean one reacts with hostility. Let's make a pact we'll honor each other's views without resorting to negative comments," he held out his hand.

His hand hung there for a long time it seemed to him. But then she slowly put out hers to grasp his. He held it and put his other hand over it. "At least, let's not be enemies."

She shook her head. "No, it's not that. It's--it's that--maybe, I'm just prickly when it comes to..."

"Men?" he finished for her.

"Let's see, you're a lawyer, PR man, a caver you said and now you're a psychologist. What else have I missed?"

He laughed. "I'd hug you if we were close and longtime friends just to show you that was said with all good intentions."

"All right," then hurriedly. "I mean, all right, I accept your good intentions. I guess we need more time to work on a friendship to make it work."

"This outing is a good time to start. I have all the time and nothing but good intentions."

He glanced at his watch. "And I've gone over my watch and kept you up. We have a lot of weekend to cram."

"My time wasn't wasted," she said. She headed back to her sleeping site.

Jeff smiled, elated, but not knowing why. He went to find his replacement.

CHAPTER NINE

Jeff's overlong watch had thrown off the subsequent watches. They had duly served their two hours, so the last one ran almost to sunrise. Or what passed for sunrise in a canyon protected by high cliffs.

John was the last one on guard and with the break of dawn and with everything as quiet as it always is in a crisp cool morning, he decided on an early investigation of the intruder.

With the heavy underbrush covering the ground, it was ridiculously easy to spot the trail leading away from the van. Carrying his Winchester at port, he followed the trail slowly, peering right and left, at the same time making as little noise as possible.

He should have awakened at least one of the sleepers and let him know where he was going. If someone woke up now and found him missing, it would alarm the group and Jean in particular. There was also the chance the intruder could circle and come into the encampment catching everyone asleep. But was this intruder dangerous? John had thought it was some curious interloper who had wandered into the area and was checking the van in order to pilfer whatever was in the vehicle.

He decided to search for another ten to fifteen minutes, then return later in the morning to resume the trail. There was a good possibility the intruder was long gone. Nevertheless, he wanted to make sure. He might come across a camp site or the remains of a fire.

He started forward and immediately brought up his rifle as he saw a figure rise up about a dozen feet away. The figure held up his hand in the universal sign of peace. Then he slowly came forward.

"Oh my God! Martin!"

"Yes, Martin, not God." He ran the final steps and embraced. "John, my son!"

When they separated, John half staggered to sit on a fallen tree trunk, shaking his head, mouth open, staring at the man.

"John, are you all right?"

John coughed, caught himself and took a deep breath, then exhaled. "You were dead! Martin, where have you been?"

"Why, right here. Waiting for you. So, where were you?"

John looked at his mentor--about five ten, gray hair with streaks of black, round face, jeans, flannel shirt, denim jacket and his University of Arizona cap. Exactly as he had seen him last. Nothing had changed--except two years.

"I don't know how to answer that, Martin. Because I could ask the same of you."

"I don't understand. There's something wrong? Who are those people? Is it the Children?"

"Yes--well, Jim and Dorothy. We never found out if the others were too."

"Jim and Dorothy are here with you? I can't wait to see them."

"In a few minutes, but first, there's others here. Ten of us altogether. Besides Jim and Dorothy and me, there are five other members of the class, including my wife and two strangers."

"You have a wife? That's wonderful. But when did that happen? The last I heard, Jim was going to appoint a judge for the group. Is that how it happened?"

"Well, yes, that judge did perform the ceremony.

"Martin was it you who blasted that hole in the mountain?"

"Yes, that was me and Daniel. Unfortunately, he got killed in the blast. I expected you and Jim sooner. But, these vehicles, where did you get them?"

"A lot of things have changed, Martin. Even so, it took some time to change them."

"Yes, there's been someone here. I found camouflage netting on the entrance. Who could have put it up? When and why?"

"I put it up with Jim's help and that of a few others."

"But--how could that be without me knowing?"

"I don't know, Martin. That's why I can't understand, where were you when we were here? We stayed a few days and certainly made enough noise."

Martin shook his head, puzzled. "I don't understand. You were here--and I didn't see or hear you?"

"Martin--what year is this?"

"What is this? You think I had a concussion from the explosion and don't know where I am? Are you going to hold up five fingers and ask me to count them?"

"Something like that. So, indulge me."

He shrugged. "Sure. It's 2020."

John sucked his breath and looked away.

"Well, wasn't that the right answer?"

"Martin," softly, "this is 2022."

Now it was Martin's turn to express shock. He sat down. "You're joking."

"I wouldn't joke about such a thing, especially to you."

"But--but how could it be?"

"That's the puzzler. Go back to yesterday--by the way, was that you last night, looking into that van?"

"Yes, I was wondering who it was. I was afraid for

the cave and its contents. Even more so since I had found that netting on the entrance."

"And that was, when?"

"Oh, four or five days ago."

"That was when you noticed the netting. And before that, what did you do?"

"Nothing, really. I was waiting for you and Jim to show up."

"How long had you been waiting?"

"Well, now I don't know after what you just told me."

"Forget about that for the time being. Tell me what you remember, at least time-wise."

"I was waiting for you, as I said. We blew up the mountain so you could bring the survivors over with the least amount of effort."

"And how long did you wait, from the time you blew up the mountain to the time you noticed the netting."

"Why--the next day," then he paused, thinking. "But if you were here for several days putting up the netting--then it doesn't make sense."

John shook his head. "Five days ago you discovered the netting and the day before that was when you blew up the mountain. In other words, according to your timetable, you blew that mountain six days ago."

"Yes--and judging by the expression on your face, there's something weird about it. Right?"

John nodded. "I can't explain it. And since you weren't aware of it, I doubt you can either.

"Let's go back and meet the others. By now they're probably wondering what happened to me?"

"I told you that cave was sacred, John. Who knows what it holds and what powers it has."

"Right now, it's something I don't want to think about. But I'm sure there's a unique adjective to describe it."

CHAPTER TEN

Jim woke up, looked at his watch: 8:20. He got up and in doing so, woke up Dorothy.

"What are you doing up so early?" she muttered.

"Well," he knelt down, kissed her and whispered in her ear, "We could zip up again and have a go at it, as the British would say."

"Let's keep them out of here. This sleeping bag ain't big enough for them, pod'na.

"Oh God!" she looked at her own watch. "It's morning already. The others will be getting up too."

"So what? This is a vacation of sorts and that's what people in love do on their vacation, stay in their room."

"Some room--ceiling unlimited, invisible walls and lumpy beds. And I'm trapped with a sex fiend."

He did an imitation of Groucho with his eyebrows. "Nothing but the best for my darling and unlike millions of couples, we don't have to worry about birth control."

She flinched. "Now that was neither humorous nor sensitive."

"Sorry, I shouldn't have put it that way. I won't ever bring up the subject again," he started to get up, but she sat up and threw her arms around him.

"No, we'll have to talk about it from time to time. You take up your frustrations in humor and that's your way. We both have to overlook and ignore any references to the subject."

He kissed her and held her in a tight embrace. Over her shoulder he could see the cave entrance and noticed there was no one there. He released her and got up. "There's no one on guard. Who was the last one?"

"I don't know. Carl, John or Oscar. Jeff was first and you were second, right?"

Jim started waking the others. He found Oscar and Carl. John was gone.

"He could be in the cave," said Jean.

Jim went to the entrance and called out. He repeated the call and there was no answer either time.

"I'll go in and look," he told the others. "Oscar, you take a look out there," he swept his arm around the area.

"I'll go with you," said Jeff. "Never go into a cave alone. That's a good practice to follow."

The search immediately became irrelevant as Oscar got their attention. "Here he comes, and there's someone else with him."

"Jim!" cried Dorothy. "It's Martin!"

Martin rushed the last few yards to embrace Jim and Dorothy.

"We thought you were dead," said Dorothy.

"Where have you been?" Jim added.

"Ah, let's discuss that later," said John. He made the introductions, keeping an eye on Martin for any reaction, but there was none he could see.

"Why don't we prepare breakfast and then we can talk, "John told them.

While the food was prepared, Martin spent the time talking to Jean. He was well acquainted with hers and John's problems in their early youth. Now from all appearances, he seemed to approve of John's choice.

So, as they ate, John explained his actions of the morning, following the trail and meeting Martin. The realization of the two men that there were two years missing in Martin's life.

The others were avid listeners and even stopped eating when the time lapse was introduced.

"It's got to be amnesia," said Sylvia to Esther, who nodded in agreement.

"Of course," Oscar put in. "Your diagnosis is based on millions and millions of woman-hours of soap opera viewing."

"Can you come up with something better?" Sylvia sniffed.

"This dynamite you set off. Were you in any way injured by the blast?" Dr. Laura asked.

"No. My ears did ring, but I was aware of what went on. Daniel was too close. Actually, he was the one who set it off. He got buried. I tried digging with my hands, but it was no use. It was too deep and I'm not sure if he was where I was trying to dig. We had brought along a pick and a shovel, but they were buried with Daniel.

"After waiting a while, I went back to the cave to wait for John or Jim to arrive. They didn't, so, I went to sleep, there in the cave.

"The next day when I woke up, I went outside and that's when I discovered the netting over the cave entrance. You know the rest."

"No, we don't know the rest, since there's two years missing," said John.

"Several days after the blast, I came here with another man, Frank Jaboty. You weren't here. I went into the cave all the way to the pool area. I didn't see you or any sign of anyone else being here.

"Later I made a return trip bringing Jean, Frank and Anna, Tom and Jane, Josh and Martha, eight of us. Again, no sign of anyone. But it was on this trip that I discovered the tablets missing."

"This cave seems to have a history of disappearing objects and people," commented Jeff.

"Now will you believe me? It's sacred," said Martin.

"If you rearrange the letters of that word, 'sacred', you come up with the word 'scared.' which is what I am right now," said Sylvia.

"It was the snakes you were afraid of, remember?" Oscar smirked.

"It's not an evil place," Martin replied. "I would have sensed it long ago."

"Which reminds me," said John. "Earlier when you saw the members of this group and shook hands, did you sense if they were also the Chosen?"

"Why--no," Martin seemed surprised. Then he looked at the others. Then he reached out and took their hands. Then he tried the same with John, Jim and Dorothy.

"Oh no!" he exclaimed. "It's gone! I can't see or feel anything."

"Even us? The three of us you earlier identified as belonging to your group of survivors?" Jim questioned.

Martin nodded, sadly.

No one said anything. Then one of the women started picking up the breakfast plates and cleaning up. The others joined in. After everything was cleaned and put away, Jim called them together.

"Martin, we all came here for a reason. Actually, John did and the rest of us joined him for a holiday outing and to give him any help we could.

"John, I think you should tell Martin about your midnight visitors. Perhaps, he can add something to the story."

So John repeated his experience with the humanoids.

"You heard my voice?" Martin was astounded. "I didn't call you--or at least I'm not aware I did. But then, with this two year lapse, I'm not sure of anything.

"Look at me. Don't I look the same as when you saw me last? Has my hair grown? Could I have been asleep or in a trance for that long? I go to sleep one night and wake up the next day, only the next day is two years later. I can't explain it. And I'm supposed to be the medicine man of the tribe."

"Amnesia is the only explanation," insisted Sylvia.

"You know there's a connection here," Jeff interjected.

"What are you talking about?" Jim asked.

"All these reports of UFO sightings, the appearance of these humanoid creatures like the ones John described, have been going on for many years. All over the planet, by all types of people from professionals to common laborers. A common thread has also emerged from these experiences, that of people being unable to account for a time loss. Later under hypnosis these people find out they've been abducted and undergone some form of medical examination. Some are even later found to have had some foreign substance injected into their bodies.

"The connection I was talking about is the humanoids John saw and Martin's time lapse. John experiences a visit from them, hears a voice that sounds like Martin, urging him to come to the cave. Well, John did. And Martin was here.

"Only the two year time lapse cannot be explained. Was he abducted?"

"But abducted for two years?"

Jeff nodded. "I've never read or heard of a period that long, but then, I haven't kept up with the goings and comings of the paranormal community. Who knows if it hasn't happened before? There's a long history of people disappearing mysteriously."

"Judge Crater and Jimmy Hoffa," said Esther.

"Yes, but those two had a background that could well explain their disappearance," Jeff nodded. "But there are many others that seem to have no reason to do so on their own."

"You're saying these people--those abducted, went through hypnosis and discovered what had happened to them during that time they couldn't account for?" the question was posed by Dr. Laura.

Jeff nodded. "Yes, under competent and supervised conditions and with professionals conducting the examination."

Laura turned to Martin. "Would you be willing to

undergo such an examination?

"I can do the hypnosis, but anyone else can be present. And we can tape the proceedings. Before you do, I would recommend a complete physical so we can eliminate any side complications. Besides, a man your age should have a physical every year. You are overdue."

Martin laughed. "All right. I'm just as anxious to clear this up as anyone else. I've never been examined by a lady doctor."

"I'll do the hypnosis and you'll be fully clothed. Perhaps Dr. Heerlson can do the physical."

"Are we going back?" Jean asked.

"There's not much more we can do out here. I wanted to check on the voice I heard and Martin showed up. So that much is accomplished."

"I thought this was a weekend to enjoy ourselves," Sylvia wailed.

"I already did," smirked Oscar. "Seeing you run out screaming in the middle of the night. Nothing in that cave can top that.

"Let's go home, Esther."

"I owe you," Sylvia shouted after him. "I won't forget.

"Every time you go to bed, you'd better look under it."

"I'm the one who does that," said Esther.

Jeff saw Martin's puzzlement over the exchange. "You'll get used to it. Just like I did."

"Children are always very playful," said Martin.

CHAPTER ELEVEN

The two couples were back in Dr. Laura's office, Jim and Dorothy, John and Jean. Again they sat in a semi-circle in front of her desk.

"I called you in early today. As you know. I'm going to have my first session with Martin. He expressed a desire to have you four present. Frankly, I'm opposed to having all of you here because it might be distracting by having you make comments or asking questions."

"I'm the latecomer here," said Jean. "John, Jim and Dorothy have had a long relationship with Martin. I'd never met him until the other day. So, there's no reason for my being here."

John placed his hand on hers. "Martin asked that you be present. He knows about our past history. He's the one who helped pick me up after..."

"After I dumped you," she finished for him.

"Yes, but somehow I think he knew that 'boy' would get 'girl' in the end.

"Anyway, he wants you here," said John.

"And we'll save our questions for later," he addressed Laura.

"Jim and I can abide by those rules," added Dorothy.

"Very well, I'll hold you to that," she said testily.

"And since we have some time before he arrives," she continued, "let's go back to our previous discussion in this office."

"You mean about not siring any offspring?" Dorothy asked.

"Yes. I'm still puzzled about what brought about your condition."

"You mean Jean's and mine?"

"Yes. You two, but also your husbands."

"We're the ones with a problem," said Dorothy. "They just need a healthy partner."

"What I meant was I'd been thinking like you. That the ones who stayed behind had the problem and that the environment was to blame."

"Well, wasn't it?" from Jean.

"I assumed; we all assumed, that their absence from the camp, even for a short while, was responsible for their not being affected like the others."

"You've found out something?" Jim asked.

"Not really. I haven't heard from Atlanta. But I realized I was taking the easy way in my reasoning. Everyone was sterile except the two who were away for a short period. Therefore, it stood to reason that something affected the class while the two were away. That was further narrowed down to the excavations which occurred while Jim and John were away. Simple, wasn't it?"

"Simple and logical reasoning," said Jim.

"Yes, but it's not proven. So we still need to explore other possibilities."

"You've lost me," said Dorothy. "I see no flaw in that logic. Those who stayed got sterile. The two who left did not."

"What I was getting at," replied Laura, "was the possibility that the two were also exposed but were not totally affected by reason of absence or other factors."

"Doesn't make sense," said John. "If that were so, why haven't the rest recovered? Our trip is the only answer."

"Ah, but sometimes you have to speculate on the impossible or the unlikely, otherwise you get trapped into thinking the easy way is the right way."

"Yes," Jim looked at her in a new light. She was a lot deeper than he first thought. Her bedside manners might be lousy, but her brains weren't passed out from behind a door.

"I see your reasoning and I applaud you not getting stuck in a rut, but I can't see what John and I did to escape or recover from the affliction, whatever it is."

"I want you and John to be more explicit and detailed on what you did while you were away. Remember, even the smallest or most trivial action might be important."

Jim nodded and leaned back. "We set out traveling southeast, or as far as we knew, it was southeast. The going was tough. The area had previously been heavily forested. Now those trees were horizontal, making us go around or over them. Also being careful not to make the wrong misstep and break or sprain your leg. I believe we traveled some two days, or maybe it was three. No major problems or incidents to mark our trip. We ended up in a box canyon, a dead end. So we decided to climb over. We couldn't see the top of the mountain, it was covered by a haze so we didn't know how high it was. As a safety precaution we tied a rope around our waists to keep us from separating in the mist and in case one of us lost our footing.

"Once we got past the haze line we could only see a few feet ahead of us. We were climbing almost blind. We finally reached the top, or what we thought was the top and only because it suddenly leveled out. It was colder and there was some snow. We figured it was too late to go back so we continued. It was about this time that John fell and took me with him. Only a jutting boulder that snagged our rope kept us from rolling all the way to the bottom. We disengaged ourselves and made it down to the other side. John got a gimpy leg. Both of us got bruises.

"At the bottom of the mountain we found ourselves in another canyon, not much different from the one we had just left. I left John to rest his leg and went looking for something he could use as a crutch. It was during this search that I came across the first marker, a series of stones placed to form an arrow pointing east. I found something John could use for a crutch and returned and told him of my discovery.

"The way that marker had been formed suggested a human presence. That it just happened to be there where we came down off the mountain, seemed contrived. But who would have known we were coming and at this precise spot? We followed the direction of the arrow since we had no preconceived plan of where to go. Before the day was over, we found several more markers. Later on, Martin would explain how he had laid out markers from several conceivable paths that led to the cave. All this in anticipation of our arrival."

"He knew or thought you would go seeking him?" Laura interrupted.

"Oh yes. He had talked to the three of us, pushing the cave as the ultimate survival shelter. So when catastrophe struck, he had no doubt we would seek out the cave.

"At any rate, we finally ran across Martin and he led us to the cave. As you have seen, he had stocked it with everything but the proverbial kitchen sink.

"We spent some time discussing the situation, his and ours and that of those remaining behind. We ate, changed clothes..."

"What did you eat?"

Jim shrugged. "Nothing exotic. Canned food, chips. Water was plentiful, cool and fresh and apparently unaffected by the catastrophe."

"You drank the water?"

"Yes. We even bathed in it. John and I had spent a lot of time there examining the tablets. Martin had built a cabin for us which we used until the winter chased us back to the reservation. Well, to where they had better quarters.

"During this time we drank the water and bathed in it. And yes, we took precautions. We bathed in the pool, but took our drinking water from where it seeped into the pool."

"Did Dorothy or any other member of the class bathe

in that pool," Laura asked.

"No. Not Dorothy, but several others made a trip there."

John answered. "Yes, we drank the water and some might have bathed in the pool. In fact, I think they did. But we were there only a few days."

"But before the disaster, both of you spent quite some time there, didn't you?" Laura continued.

"Yes, several months. The summer and part of the fall of 2019," Jim replied.

"All right, continue with your journey."

"Well, if you're looking for something significant that would affect us physically, there isn't more.

"We went looking for a shorter way to connect with our classmates, but there wasn't. For a while we considered using the river, but the current was too swift and it was going in the opposite direction.

"We did find the body of Betty Leye, one of our classmates left behind, and that made it imperative that we return as soon as possible. So, we finally went back the way we came. Martin suggested blowing up the mountain. He had a case of dynamite. And eventually he did, which led us to believe he might have been killed in the blast.

"After that we crossed the mountain and had a fight with this survivalist group, one of whom had captured Dorothy and after that a fire fight at the base of the mountain. Then Martin blew it and buried most of the bad guys. Nothing more that affected us physically except that I got wounded on my head and back, but not seriously.

"And that about tells it all."

"This water in the cave," Laura came on, "how did it taste? Any aftereffects after drinking it?"

"What can I say? It was cool like water coursing through the limestone to finally come out at that pool. John?"

John shook his head. "Can't say there was anything outstanding about it. And no aftereffects that I recall."

"You think that water might have something to do with our condition?" said Jim.

"Seems to be the only thing out of the ordinary that

you did--and you did it for quite some time. Several months as opposed to a few days some of the others did."

"Are we getting back to the supernatural--UFOs, alien creatures and now magical waters?" Dorothy grinned.

"Why not?" Laura smiled. "There are springs with high contents of sulphur that people claim have healing powers."

"And don't forget Lourdes," said Jean.

"So you think the water had something to do with it?" Jim asked.

"I won't say that without more conclusive evidence. All I'm saying is that the water you ingested seems to be the only foreign substance that entered your bodies. Everything else you did was something you could have done anywhere, any time."

"Including getting shot?" Jim laughed.

"An everyday affair," she brushed it off. "Just visit the emergency center of any hospital."

"Then you want to follow up this, supposedly water mystery?" Jim asked.

"Yes I would. In fact, it might be a good idea to test Martin too. I know he's a lot older, but men older than him have fathered children, so it wouldn't hurt to try. Do you think he spent enough time there, using the pool in the cave?"

"Yes, I know that for a fact," said John.

"Good, that could clinch it."

"Suppose that Jean and I go there and drink and bathe," Dorothy spoke up. "Over a time, do you suppose..."

"There's no harm trying," Laura looked kindly at the two women, "but at the same time don't get your hopes up too high. It's only a theory, a possibility."

"Yeah, Carl has a theory about my midnight visitors," said John.

There was a knock on the door. Laura didn't answer John. She went and opened the door.

Martin peeked in. "I'm here." He came in, followed by Jeff Randall.

"What's he doing here?" Laura asked, crossly.

"Ah, my friend, my new pal," said Jeff. "How fast I've made friends here."

"It's not that," she pleaded. "This session was supposed to be private and confidential. Now it threatens to explode like a media circus."

"I asked Jeff to join us," said Martin.

"And you also asked these four," she rejoined

She threw up her hands. "All right. It's your life you're going to make public. But I warn you," she turned to the others, "If you don't cooperate out you go."

CHAPTER TWELVE

"This couch looks so comfortable I could fall asleep," said Martin.

"That's the idea," said Laura, "although not sleep as you generally defined it.

"Relax. Look at the light on the camcorder. Breath normally. Not a care in the world. If you see or hear anything that is disagreeable or that you fear, you will come back to the present time at once. Understand that? Remember that.

"Relax. Go deep," she continued. To the side a camcorder whirred recording sight and sound. Behind her, sitting quietly, were the invited guests.

"For the record, give me your name and date of birth and a brief history of your background."

"My name is Martin Hill and I was born on July 11th 1958. I served in the military in the 70s, then I got a couple of degrees at the University of Arizona. I am the shaman of my tribe and sit on the tribal council board. The president with the advice and consent of the board runs the affairs of the tribe. The tribe has several businesses, like cattle ranches, fishing and hunting resorts..."

"All right," she interrupted. "Relax, let's go deeper. We're at the year 2019. Anything of significance happen then?"

"Yes! Yes! Finally, after so many years that I had begun to despair, to doubt my heritage--and of all things, in the form of a white man.

"John brought him to me in all innocence--or perhaps it wasn't. Perhaps it was ordained.

"A white man was one of us, one of the Chosen. I couldn't believe it, but it was true. I saw it; I felt it. Right away I told him. I couldn't contain myself. But he didn't believe it, of course. But he was polite while voicing his disbelief.

"It wasn't until John and I took him to the cave and showed him the tablets that he became excited."

"All right," she interrupted again. "Let's jump into the next year, 2020. Again, what significant event occurred?"

"The end came, just as I always said. We were in the cave..."

"You survived and you were left alone?"

"No. Daniel also made it, but later he got killed setting off the explosion. But that's a little ahead. John and Jim made it over the mountain and found me and the cave. When they had to return, there was no other way except over the mountain again. So I decided to blow a path through it to make it easier when they returned with the others. So we blew the mountain, but Daniel got killed."

"So that done, what did you do then?"

"Well, I just waited for John and Jim to return"

"Did they come right away? That explosion should have told them you had opened a path for them."

"No--I didn't expect them that soon. They had to gather their people and their supplies."

"All right. What then?"

"I went back to the cave. I was going to wait for them there. They knew the way."

"And? At the cave, what happened?"

"Nothing. I ate and then went to sleep after dark."

"Anything happen that night? Or any other night?"

"No," he paused.

"Are you sure? I want you to go deeper and deeper."

"Yes, I..." he gasped. "Who are they?"

"What? What do you see?"

"These--these little people."

"What do they look like?"

"They're small--well, they're about this high," he brought his hand to his chest.

"Oh, about four feet or so," she said.

"Anything else that you can describe?" she continued.

"They're grayish looking--but it's those eyes. So big and black."

"You're in the cave you said and it's night, so how can you see?"

"The fire. I have a fire. It's low now but I'm camped close to the entrance. There's enough light to see."

"What do they want? Do they say anything?"

"No, they're just looking at me. Maybe it's the ghosts of my ancestors--No, wait, he said something."

"He? You said little people. How many are there?"

"There's two of them, but he--they don't speak, but I hear it."

"What do you hear?"

"He said--or they said.' You are coming with us.'"

"You said they didn't speak, but you heard them. How do you explain that?"

"I don't know. I just heard it--in my head."

"All right. So what are you doing?"

"I don't want to go--and I tell them so. It doesn't matter. They're taking me. These little people, they just lifted me up and taking me."

"They lifted you with their hands?"

"No--Oh God! I'm just suspended in mid-air."

Laura was getting just as excited, but she forced herself to remain calm. "Where are they taking you? Tell me what you see or hear."

"They're taking me into the cave. I can't move or

struggle against them. We're--Look out! We're going to hit the--" gasp. "We went through the cave wall!"

There was a murmur from the back of the room, but Laura waved it down without taking her eyes from her subject.

"You were carried straight through a cave wall? Did you feel anything?"

"No. That's funny. We're going through rock and I don't feel anything. I must be dreaming."

"Are you? "

"I don't know. Only in dreams do these crazy things happen. But I don't think I would dream of going through rock."

"So you've been taken through rock. Where are you now or have you reached where they were taking you?"

"It's dark. I'm going--or maybe I'm floating. I don't feel anything--you know, like ground under your feet.

"There! I see it!"

"What?"

"Oh no! A UFO. A spaceship. This has to be a dream."

"Is that what you see?"

"I can't believe it. Those things are not supposed to exist except in science fiction."

"Can you touch it? Maybe it's like those cave walls, you can go through it."

"I'm walking to it. They've let me go, but they're watching me."

"What have they told you? What do they want from you?"

"Nothing--they've said nothing.

"Ah--it's real. The ship is real--at least I think so. It feels like metal. But maybe it's their doing, a dream or an illusion."

"Are you still in the cave? Is that where the ship is?"

"Yes--Well, maybe--It's a chamber--in the cave, I guess. The hanger for the ship. It's about the size of a small house.

"Huh, it's the plain everyday UFO someone is always

reporting as buzzing their front yard. Circular, looks dark, but maybe because it's dark in here. No lights--but maybe they don't come on until it's running.

"They're coming for me. They say we have to go."

"Where?"

"We have to go--That's all. They don't say where."

"Are you afraid?"

"Yes--but excited--if this is all true. I keep thinking it's a dream because only dreams are this crazy. There! A hatch is opening. They're taking me in--I don't want to, but I don't seem to have a choice.

"I'm floating again--into the ship. They're putting me in this seat, this chair. Now they put on belts on me."

"They're tying you?"

"It's like a seatbelt. They're saying not to be afraid. That's the first time they've said anything nice."

"They're talking now?"

"Not like us. You know, in my head.

"There's a humming sound now."

"What kind of humming? Can you tell?"

He shrugged. "It's just humming."

"Are they still there? Are you alone?"

"Not close by. I can see them. But--oh, I see two other people like me--humans--they're sitting in a chair like me I--Oh, it's taking off--the ship--I can feel it pressing me down on the seat."

"Is there a window you can see out?"

"No--wait, now--it's stopping. I don't feel it pressing down any more."

"Did it land or is it like an airplane reaching cruising speed?"

"I don't know. If it's flying, it's the smoothest trip I ever took. They're coming back--taking off the belt."

Silence.

"Go on. What's happening now?"

"They've taken me to another room. It's like a doctor's examining room, only there's several tables. They've got the other two humans here too.

"No! They want me to take off my clothes--No, I

don't want to--Oh--they're doing it for me--putting me on the table. Oh, I don't like this. They're strapping me to the table."

"All right, relax. You're going to get through this."

"There's another one of the little people. I think he wants to play doctor." Martin was breathing heavily.

"It's all right," Laura tried to reassure him. "Remember..."

"It's coming down--from the ceiling--like a shaft, a needle--Oh no!"

He screamed.

CHAPTER THIRTEEN

Laura was on her feet. "No! No!--It's over. You're coming back. Remember what I told you. Slowly--On the count of three--one--They're gone--two--You're on the way back--three--Open your eyes. You're back home--With your friends."

John had rushed to Martin's side. Now he took his hand.

"We're here, Martin."

Martin's eyelids were fluttering, his breathing ragged.

Laura was affixing a blood pressure strap on his arm.

"Relax, you're safe now. It's over."

"You're fine now, Martin," John assured him. "I think that's enough for today," he glanced at Laura.

"Yes. Let's give you a break. Just rest there for a while. Let me check your blood pressure."

"What happened?" Martin looked at the faces around him. "It wasn't good, was it? I can tell by your faces. Did I make a fool of myself?"

“No, you didn't," Laura told him. "You were reliving

an unpleasant episode. It was like a bad dream."

"You mean a nightmare."

"We all have them--and we get over them," she was pumping the blood pressure device.

He turned his head to watch it. "Am I higher than the Dow?"

"Not quite. It's high, but understandable under the circumstances. I'll check again later when you've settled down."

He sat up and took in the others. "How did I do?"

"It's all on the tape," said Jim, "and in glorious living color."

"Shall we see it?" Martin glanced around the circle of faces.

"We have already seen it--live," said Dorothy.

"Why don't we go over it tomorrow," said Laura.

"Can we take him home?" John asked.

"Of course. Come in tomorrow at nine. We'll see how he's doing."

"I'm doing fine, Doctor. I'm the healthiest sixty year old in the country."

"You're sixty two, Martin," John corrected him.

"I don't feel it."

"Yeah, what's two years," John winked at the others. John took Martin by his arm, Jean on the other side and they left.

"Abduction!" said Jeff as the door closed behind them.

"Yes--so? What is that supposed to prove?" Laura returned his look.

"God, woman! Must you always work at being irritating 100% of the time?"

They seemed oblivious that Jim and Dorothy were still there.

"Is this a private fight or can anyone put in their two cents?" Dorothy cracked.

"Two cents is two cents more than this is worth," he turned to leave, but Jim grabbed his arm.

"Look you two, I thought you had made your peace

back at the cave," he took in both of them.

"It doesn't matter, Jim. When this is over, let me know the outcome of Martin's chronicles." He left.

Dorothy turned to Laura. "He said 'abduction' and you sneered at his observation. Let up, Laura. What's your problem?"

Laura sat down and put her hands to her face. "I took it out on him. I could have done that to you or the Edlemans, but he was the convenient target. Martin's reaction scared me. I thought I had done something wrong--and maybe I did. So I picked on Jeff. I'm sorry."

"You're apologizing to the wrong person," said Dorothy.

"Jeff just separated himself from this investigation," said Jim. "I got the idea Martin was very gung ho about including him in these sessions. I hope you can come up with an explanation he will accept. "Dorothy, shall we go?"

She nodded, put her hand on Laura's shoulder and they left her alone.

Laura put both hands on the table then dropped her head on them.

Jeff got to his room, slamming the door shut. What is wrong with that woman?--Or was it him? He remembered her flare-up had come against him. He had mentioned 'abduction' and she had pinned him to the wall as if he had said a dirty word. It was like two substances that just naturally repelled each other. But no, only one was repelled. The other was just puzzled and with no explanation why the two couldn't mix.

Back at the cave he had been delighted that their differences had been settled. Or so he had thought. She had been nettled at his appearance at the session with Martin. And now this latest outburst.

She was a very attractive woman and a professional. Certainly it didn't seem out of character for two people to be friends, especially since they were outsiders. True, the people had been very friendly and had accepted them. There were other women from the class who were single and attractive, but she was the one he had felt drawn to. But every meeting between the two, except that one time at the cave, had produced sparks of the negative kind.

Martin's experience was a subject in which he had always had an interest. He had read extensively about it in his earlier years. Even now, every new theory or revelation caught his attention. So he stored up new reports relating to it. This was the first time he had been involved first hand. He hated bowing out, but saw no way out that couldn't cause friction.

He would make his excuses to Martin. Or just don't show up. He could say his duties would take up all his time. An excuse sure to draw a snort of derision from the good doctor. Maybe he should return to Washington and tell the congressman he wanted out. Resign. He hated the thought because he liked it here and saw the challenge facing these people and he wanted to be a part of it.

On the other hand, should he let one person control his life and force him to abandon what he wanted to do?

His thoughts were interrupted by a knock on the door. He opened the door and Laura came through without being asked.

"Please come in," he said, sarcastically.

"I was afraid you would slam the door on my face."

"Now, what gave you that idea?"

"I deserve that. And more. That's why I'm here. I'm sorry. Please accept my apologies."

"Wow! Laura Criden apologizing to me. Have you been abducted by an alien and brainwashed? Really, I don't know how to answer or acknowledge that without provoking a tart reply."

"All right. You've had you fun. I got it coming. And speaking of tart replies, you haven't done so bad yourself. But I'm still standing. They haven't knocked me down. Sure, I deserve a kick in the ass. I'm swallowing my pride and anything else you can think of in making my apology."

"I'll make it easy for you. Obviously the Fenzers have been talking to you, but I hope you didn't do it just for them.

So I'll accept it. But what about the next time?

"I can tell you right now that no apologies are necessary. There's something about me that makes your hair stand on end. You can't fight that. So I'll make it easy for you. I'll stay out of your way. I'll talk to my boss about replacing me. You're needed more. You're a doctor."

"No, no. That's why I'm here. Not only to apologize, but to urge you to remain a part of this team."

"You mean with Martin? Or this Stonecliff project?"

"Judging by all we've heard, I think it's obvious they all tie together.

"Everyone is sterile except the two men who spent a lot of time in or near that cave. So did Martin. And Martin was abducted from there."

"By creatures who may call it home."

"Yes. Always assuming what we heard was true. That's another reason I want your input. You seem familiar and up-to-date in this phenomena."

"Oh, you want my brain and not my body?"

She grimaced, her eyes narrowing. "Don't make me change my mind."

"I was testing you. You have to relax and see the humorous side. You know, Laura. Getting along with people means understanding who they are. I'm not a doctor or a scientist, but at the risk of offending you again, you need to lighten up."

She looked at him, her mouth a grim line, but she saw a trace of a smile on his face. She relaxed.

"All right. I'll go even further. I'm insecure. How's that confession for a doctor of medicine? That's why I lashed out at you. Did I do something wrong to bring out that scream from Martin? Indians are supposed to be stoic. Unafraid of the unexpected. I"m not an expert in this hypnosis field. In fact, this is the first time I've done this. The night before I had to cram all I could on this subject. So please understand how I felt."

"I see," he nodded. "As you said, you're insecure—and you're a woman. So that puts a big burden on your shoulders.

“You have to make good not only for your self-confidence, but also for all womanhood. May I ask another intrusive question? Is this Stonecliff project your first one on your own?"

"Yes."

He nodded. "And since the success of your project depends on staying on good terms with these people, you can't afford to take out your frustrations on them. As an outsider I was a better target for your darts."

"Are you a psychologist now?"

"No, but don't we all try to act like one? And sometimes even amateurs come close in their diagnosis. Look, I'm not unsympathetic. I'm trying hard to understand you so there won't be another blow-up. I want to think I did all I could to avoid that."

"And you have. You've been completely innocent in these blow-ups, as you call them--See I've already made progress. I've taken responsibility for my mistakes. So don't back off this project because of me. I want you to come back and I'm sure Martin wants you included in the sessions."

"Only because of that?"

"What else do you want me to do? Get on my knees?"

"I'm tempted to answer that with a frivolous remark, but I'll pass. You've just graduated into the human race. You need more experienced in repartee with a veteran like me."

"Oh? I'm trembling in the presence of one so wise with the knowledge of the ages at the tip of his tongue."

"Oh, I like that. Would it strain our new-found relationship if I asked you to lunch?"

"No. I think we need further talks on bedside manners and winning friends and influencing people. You seem to be the self-appointed expert."

"Way to a man's heart is through his stomach."

"I wasn't planning to go that far.

"You're paying, of course."

"Wouldn't have it any other way. You know me, the macho type. I'll find my way wherever it leads me."

“Yeah, yeah. C’mom, big spender.”

CHAPTER FOURTEEN

Jim and Dorothy arrived late the next morning at Dr. Laura's office. The rest were already there, that is, those who had set in yesterday's session with Martin.

"Sorry," said Dorothy. "We had to get our people at the store going on today's project."

"All right," replied Laura, irritably. "But remember, you're invited guests. We can go on without you."

"No we won't," said Martin. "Jim and Dorothy are very much included in any plans involving me."

Laura stared at him, then took in the others. "This is a closed corporation, I see."

"No, it's not closed," said John. "We voted you and Jeff in some time ago."

"And you haven't stopped to notice," added Jean.

"A career does not a whole life make," Dorothy agreed.

Laura turned to Jeff. "When do I hear from you?"

"You already have--remember?"

"It looks like I'm outnumbered."

"Wrong answer," said Dorothy. "But, you're right to some extent. This is not the time for a discussion on relationships."

Laura expelled her breath. "All right then. We're going to go over yesterday's session. Mostly to allow Martin to view it. If Martin has some comments to make along the way,

"I'll stop the tape and we'll discuss it. Then if Martin is up to it, we'll go into the second session at the point where we left off.

"Any comments before we start?"

"Yes," John spoke up. "How much does Martin remember or is aware of? From yesterday's events, I mean, since he was under hypnosis."

"I didn't implant a suggestion that he remember everything. But, is that what you want?" turning to Martin.

"Let me look and hear myself first. I'll give you an answer before we start again."

There were no more questions, so Laura started the tape. All the visual effects were of Martin lying on the couch, so only his voice and Laura's made a difference.

No comments were forthcoming until Martin mentioned little people. "Oh boy," said Martin softly.

Then when they went through the cave wall. "I guess I'm a candidate for a visit to a shrink."

No one replied.

When he mentioned the UFO, or spaceship, he just glanced, nervously at the others, but made no comment.

As the tape ended with his scream, he got up and went to stand by the window.

Laura turned off the tape. Everyone was silent.

"We don't have to continue this if you don't want to," she said.

"Oh no! We must go on," Martin turned from the window.

"That cave has been an important part of my life. I don't know if we can ever discover all the secrets hidden there. But I have to know as much as I can. Maybe under hypnosis I can supply my own answers."

Laura nodded. "Let's get started then. Lie down. Look at the red light on the camcorder. Relax. Take a deep breath. Now exhale. You're going deep. Afterwards, you will remember everything. We will go back to that point where we left off. But immediately after that experience with the needle. It didn't harm you. Did it? You're here. Did it have any other effect on you?"

"No--I guess not. It was like a physical. I got worse in the army. In the army they stuck needles in me from every direction in all my three years with them."

"Yes, yes. Now tell me what is happening."

"Like I said. It is like a physical. They're sticking and poking at me. They're--you know--down there. They probably took some samples."

"What do you think they were checking you for? Did they say anything?"

"They don't say anything," he grunted. "They're men of few words--well, if they're men--or at least as we think of men."

"You can tell the gender?"

"Well, I get the impression they were male. I could be wrong. There's really no physical indication of their sex that I can see."

"Are you alone? Is there anyone else?"

"Well--yes, there are at least two other people like me. They're at another table like me. One of them is a woman.

She has long hair and I can see her--ah, chest."

"What are they doing?"

"To her?"

"Yes."

"Giving her a physical like me. You know, like when they check for a baby."

"Ah--they checked you and her more or less for the same thing--your reproductive abilities."

"Yeah. Can you imagine that? A sixty year old man like me. I guess that's a compliment."

"Yes, let's call it that and move on. If nothing of importance came out of the examination, then you're through. What happened then?"

"They're taking me off the table. My clothes are being handed back. They're leading me back to the chair and strapping me down again."

"They are bringing you back, then?"

"Yes--Well, that's what I hope. Once more I feel pressed down on my seat. But when the pressure slackened, we don't stop. I feel funny."

"Funny? Describe funny."

"Dizzy--head spinning--Achy. God! I feel like dying!"

"Did you feel nauseous or feel like vomiting?"

"Yeah, but one of them came over and put his hand on my neck. He said it will pass."

"People feel that way when they get airsick."

"I don't know. It just feels awful."

"All right. Let's skip to where the feeling stops."

"It stopped. The feeling, I mean. I'm still on the ship."

"What's happening now?"

"They're coming for me--It's time to go they say."

"Go where?"

"They didn't say--No--they took off the belt and they're taking me again. It must--Oh, oh, the hatch is open. I can see daylight ahead."

"So they dropped you outside instead of inside the cave?"

"Yes--And the other two people, a man a woman. The ones I saw on the ship."

"Oh?" Laura was confused. "There were two other people, a couple, who were released the same time you were? Why are they releasing you together if only you were picked up?"

"I don't know. I don't ask and they aren't saying."

"They take you, then. Where are you? Do you recognize the place?"

"No, but it's nice. The weather is just fine. I can see mountains in the distance. There's trees, a meadow. I can see a house in the distance. There also seem to be some farm animals. I can't tell what kind from this distance."

"What do your captors say? What do they do?"

"Nothing--They left us there. They went back to the ship. It's taking off."

"What now? What do you and this couple do?"

"We're walking towards the house we saw."

"Does the other couple say anything?"

"No. We started towards the house by mutual consent."

"Go on."

"We're at the house. There's four people watching us. Actually two adults and two children, about seven and nine."

"What do they say? What did anyone say?"

"Nothing for a while. Then I ask where we are.

"'Don't you know?' says the man.

"I wouldn't be asking if I knew. I was in Arizona, sleeping, when the little people took me.

"'Are you an Indian?' the little girl asks.

"Yes, are you Americans?

"'We're from Ohio.' says the man.

"This doesn't look like Ohio, I say. I never saw mountains that high in Ohio.

"'No, this isn't Ohio.' says the man. 'There's no place to go from here. In Ohio there would be a road close by and that road would lead to a town.'

"I look at his house--it is a log cabin, actually. Maybe one big room. This looks like nineteenth century America.

"How did you get here if there are no roads?

"He pointed to the sky, 'The same way you did. They brought me--us.'

"I look around his place. I see a corral with two horses, beyond on the meadow, I see about a dozen cows. 'Did they get here the same way?'

"He nodded. 'We woke up one morning and there were tools and clothes and food. All we needed to get by. Then they left the livestock. There's chickens and hogs around.'

"'Then you've got everything you need,' I told him.

"'Everything except family, friends and neighbors.'

"'How long have you been here'?

"'I don't know. We lost track. Back home, the last I remember, it was 2019.'

"'Then you've been gone over a year. It's 2020.'

"His wife started crying and so did the kids.

"'Don't feel bad, I told them. In Arizona, there was a tremendous catastrophe. As far as I know, the rest of the country or even the world may not be the same.'

"'Oh, I know about that,' said the man who had come with me. 'I'm from Kansas and that was all over the news. But it was only in Arizona, Utah and New Mexico.'

"That was news to me. So it hadn't been the end of the world.

"'I'm Richard and this is Rebecca.' said the man who had been left with me. 'I don't know what this is about. Why did they take us and where are we?'

"The man who had greeted us said, 'We're the Tolands.

I'm Nate, this is Sarah and Gwen and Terrence. And I still can't tell you where we are.'

"'Martin Hill,' I said and we shook hands all around. 'It looks like somewhere out West.' The other two were Richard and Rebecca Anders.

"'There's mountains like that in many parts of the world.' said Richard. 'And the weather could be anywhere from spring to fall.'

"'The weather is like this all the time.' said Nate.

"'Do you know why we are here?' I asked.

"'I don't know.' said Nate. 'But they seem to be keeping track of us. They've brought us everything we need to stay alive. That's the good part. Everything else we don't care about.'

"'So this is permanent'? asked Richard.

"'Who knows. You all say this is the year 2020. Maybe my next visitor will say its 2023 or 2025.'

"It's not something I want to hear. Neither did Richard and Rebecca."

Laura had been letting Martin go on, fascinated with the turn of events. So were the others.

Now she cut in. "When they first took you into the

spaceship, they sat you down and buckled you to the seat.

“You said you felt pressed down to the chair. Would that be because the ship was taking off and accelerating?"

"Yes, that's a good comparison."

"Then after they finished your examination, they buckled you in the seat again and you felt the same acceleration?"

"Yes--except for that funny feeling."

"Were you ever able to look out a window or port on this ship?"

"No. I was never close to any windows."

"So you don't know where they took you for your examination or where you went afterwards?"

"No--Well, I didn't see the direction. It was after they landed and they left that we had any idea where we were."

"And where were you?"

"Like I said. It had to be somewhere in the West. It makes sense."

"From the time you felt the acceleration until you landed, how long do you estimate the time of your flight?"

"That's hard to say--maybe ten to fifteen minutes."

"All right. Let's go back to where you landed and the people there. Did they go through the same procedure as you did? I mean the examination and then being dropped in this unknown location?"

"Yes, they told me that later."

"All right. So how long were you there with the Tolands?"

"A long time. After a while we tried to keep track. The aliens brought us many things including writing materials. So we set an approximate time and made a calendar. We still had our watches, but they had stopped when we were abducted. And how long would our batteries last?"

"And according to your calendar, how long were you there?"

"Almost two years. There were some problems with the time. I felt like the days were longer. But the climate never changed. It was ideal. We couldn't believe it."

"Do you still think you were somewhere out West?"

"I had nothing else to compare."

"All right. Let's leave that for later discussion. Tell me of any significant events while you were there?"

"Nothing much. With us there, the Tolands seem to be happier. They finally had someone to talk to. All of us pitched in and we built a house for Richard and Rebecca."

"What are their last names?"

"Only one. Anders. They're married."

"What about you? Did you build a home?"

"Actually, yes. I built a Hogan for myself. The kids got a big kick out of it. A real Indian among them."

"So you built a home and lived happily ever after. Or did you?"

"As well as I could."

"What did you do with your time besides building homes and entertaining the kids?"

"I tried to find out more of our surroundings. I took trips. It is beautiful country. I even found game. But I didn't find any signs of human habitation. I think I went out some fifty, sixty miles. I made it to the top of that mountain, actually part of a range. Beautiful, as far as I could see. But no sign of anyone but me."

"How do you feel about this--I mean, being stranded?"

"Like I said, it was beautiful country, rough and wild. I have no complaints. I often wondered about my friends I left behind. But I had no control. I am willing to accept spending the rest of my life here. Oh, the explorations I can make. Maybe with Terry when he gets older."

"How about the Anders and the Tolands? What is their thinking?"

"They are younger and used to having more civilization around. I know they miss that and their families. The Tolands have been here longer and getting used to it. The kids are adapting better than the parents. It won't be easy but they'll make it."

"Let's get to your final day there."

"I was on a trip of discovery. Long ago I had figured

we were all alone, at least for a hundred mile radius. The Tolands and the Anders were farming, so they weren't much for making such expeditions. I went by myself. I enjoyed it. It was the closest thing to home. Perhaps better, since some of our tribe had too much civilization and had forgotten the old ways. Many could only track their way to the nearest liquor store.

"I had gone out for three or four days. I picked a direction and set out. I had all 360 degrees of the compass to choose. Everywhere I went I marked the trail, not only to find my way back, but also on the slim possibility there were other people out there looking for our company. I acted like a vandal, leaving my name on tree trunks and rocks. Someday, people might know I had been there.

"On the second night, it happened. They came. Again, two of them. 'Where are we going this time,' I asked.

"'You're going back home to your friends.'

"'They know where I am. I'll see them in two days.'

"They didn't say anything more, but floated me off to their spaceship. I was used to it by now.

"So I went through the same routine, only backwards. Then they brought me back to the cave. 'You will remember everything. Tell your friends.'

"That's when I woke up. My memory was wiped out which didn't make sense because they told me to remember every-thing."

"Yes, we know the rest. And apparently they knew that somehow, your memory would be restored.

"We'll end the session now. You will remember everything you have experienced. On the count of three--one, you are coming out of your deep trance. Two, you are almost here. You can feel life returning to your limbs. You want to stretch. Three, you are back in Stonecliff with your old friend."

CHAPTER FIFTEEN

Laura stopped the recording and turned on the lights as Martin came to. He sat up and turned to look at his friends.

"How did I do?"

"Great!" exclaimed Jeff. "Laura, I think you should keep the tape going to discuss the implications of Martin's story."

Laura nodded and restarted the recording.

Dorothy glanced at Jean and whispered. "Are we seeing a breakthrough here?"

"She's almost submissive," Jean replied.

"If I might start out," said Jeff. "And at the risk of sounding pretentious, I've followed the UFO, alien abduction controversy pretty close. There's dozens if not hundreds of stories like Martin's out there. One more isn't going to cause any stir. Not that I think we ought to publicize it now--or maybe ever. That's up to Martin as the main player and Dr. Criden as the interrogator. It might hurt her career with certain elements of her profession.

"It's always been almost impossible to prove the truth of these alien experiences. It's usually based only on the testimony of one person who saw and/or heard something and which many times is not remembered until brought out by hypnosis. An art which many view with suspicion if not outright disbelief.

"In the victim's defense, it's been said that these people have no reason to bring attention to themselves and have nothing to gain by it. But sooner or later, they feel a loss of time or a nagging feeling that something is not right. A hidden experience waiting to come out. Then they seek medical help or someone suggests a shrink. Eventually through these sessions, their experiences are bared to the astonishment of the interrogator, not to mention disbelief.

“Then comes the book and the TV interviews to promote it, written by the interrogator, sometimes with the help and permission of the victim.

"There's more to this genre, but it's unimportant at this point.

"In Martin's story, I don't know how many of you caught the one item that can make this more than one person's story of I-saw or I-heard," he stopped and looked at the others.

"No," said Dorothy, "but I think you're busting to tell us."

Jeff flushed. "Yeah, I deserve that. I guess my enthusiasm slip is showing. But this is the first time that we have a clue to investigate the authenticity of this experience.

"Martin mentioned the names of these two families, the Tolands and the Anders. He gave us the name of their home states. If they have been gone since 2019 and 2020, respectively, then it's a good bet they should be on a Missing Person's List for those states and maybe even nationwide."

"Yes, that's a good observation," said Jim. "How do you go about verifying that without arousing suspicion on why you want to know? We're talking about people disappearing two and three years ago. Why would someone in Arizona be interested they could ask? And how about their relatives?

“Do you arouse their interest now after they have accepted, I would hope, their disappearance? What do you tell them? Not Martin's story, I would hope."

"No, we can't go that route," Jeff agreed. "You can't drop the information that you learned about them in a hypnosis session. They would probably suspect a scam of some sort."

"Wouldn't that information be in a computer and available to all police departments?" said John.

"Of course," Jeff snapped his fingers. "I'll go to the congressman's office and get a list. And in order not to arouse suspicion, I'll just ask for a list of the entire year for each state."

"That could be a lengthy list," said Jim.

"Possibly. I have no idea how many people go on such list in a year's time. It doesn't matter. Once we get the list, there's enough of us here that can go over it. It shouldn't take more than a few hours. I'll call Washington today and get them to send the lists to me."

"You'd better have a story to back that request in case your boss gets curious," said John.

"The 2020 case should be easy since that's when the disaster occurred. We can say we believe they were related to a citizen of Stonecliff. In fact, we could say the same for the Tolands."

"But it's now 2022." said John. "If they had relatives here and the Tolands disappeared in 2019, their relatives in Stonecliff would have been aware of their disappearance."

"True," replied Jeff. "But the rest of us wouldn't know that. Now searching through the debris of early Stonecliff civilization, we have come across artifacts that indicate the Tolands may have had some ties to this community."

"Hmm. Lying seems to come so easy," said Laura. "But I guess it could work."

"Is it important to verify it?" Martin asked.

"You're the one who said it could all be a crazy dream," Laura reminded him. "Let's find out if it is."

"The next question that comes to mind is, where was

Martin? The country that looks like the West," Jim said.

"Uh-huh," said Jeff. "I'm curious, especially that you had temperate weather all the time. That's unheard of except in tropical areas. You certainly weren't in the South Seas, were you?"

"Not that I know of," Martin was puzzled. "As I said I covered a radius of over a hundred miles. That was no island I was on. And while the area was wild and rough, it was no jungle. The vegetation didn't look tropical. No monkeys or coconuts in the trees."

"You said your trip in this UFO took from ten to fifteen minutes. You were in Arizona," Jeff looked at him. "How far can you go in that time from Arizona?"

"I think you both are forgetting one thing," said Jim. "You're not talking about an ordinary aircraft here. All I've ever heard of UFOs is their tremendous speed. In ten or fifteen minutes, for all we know, a UFO could cross the Milky Way."

Jeff's face fell. "Damn! You're right. I forgot that."

"Maybe," Laura glanced at him, "that UFO made a stop while crossing the Milky Way. Hasn't there always been speculation that there are other stars with habitable planets? If we're going to guess, why not that? Could it be that these little people dropped these humans on a planet that was compatible and on which they could survive?"

Everyone looked at her in astonishment.

"That's the most intelligent assessment made all day," said Jeff. "I've been going in all directions with long monologues and the lady comes in with the best and in a few words."

Dorothy whispered to Jean. "Someone is trying to make brownie points."

"Let's try to organize this," said Jim. "First, why abduct Martin and these other people? Were they chosen for a reason or at random? Having been abducted, they are examined with close attention to their reproductive parts. Why is that important? Then why drop them in this place, wherever it is and leave them there? They weren't forgotten or left to die. These aliens supplied them with all they needed to survive. Finally, why did they return Martin, but not the others? Martin was the one most happy and able to adjust to the new environment while the others missed their old life and would have been happier to return."

Laura went to a blackboard she had in her office and erased it clean.

"Let's suppose," she said as she drew two circles, one on each side of the board, "that one represents Earth and the other Planet X, wherever in the heavens it's at. They pick up the people and examine them and prepare them for a trip to Planet X. You could compare it to a soldier going overseas. Carrying that analogy further, the soldier gets shipped to his new station along with the supplies and equipment to sustain him."

"Seems to me," Dorothy interjected, "that this sounds more like a colonizing project."

"Exactly," Laura agreed. "Except for Martin. They drop these families on this planet, leave sufficient supplies, and then let nature take its course. And they made sure these people are capable of reproducing. So you're right, Dorothy. It looks more like a colonizing effort than establishing a beachhead or an invasion."

"So why Martin?" John asked.

"Yes, why Martin?" Laura looked at the others. "Let's discuss that. Was he an accidental pickup? Doesn't make sense. He was alone in this cave. If they wanted people to colonize a planet, why pick a single, overaged man in a cave?"

"Oh my God!" Dorothy exclaimed.

"What?" from Jim.

"A thought just crossed my mind. What has Martin been preaching and pushing since we've known him? The Chosen. The First Children. The ones who would survive to populate the new world."

"We won't pass the physical," said Jean.

"I never thought of it that way," said Martin, thoughtfully.

"Are they using you as a recruiter?" Jim asked.

"No--at least I'm not conscious of it. I have no reason

to push anyone to go there. I don't know where it is even if I wanted to."

"Unless they implanted the idea in your head and it's set to go off at a time convenient to them," said Jim.

"I can't swear to that either way," replied Martin. "I was under their control. They could have done what they wanted with me--and they did."

"I don't fancy being a pioneer in some far-off planet," commented Jean.

"You may not have much to say about it," said Laura. "They seem to have the ability to take anyone regardless of the personal wishes of the abductee."

"That's right," Martin agreed. "Myself, the Tolands and the Anders were not willing passengers on their spaceships or where we landed."

"And it makes me wonder if they are through with you," said Jeff. "According to written accounts of these abductions, the victims keep getting abducted over and over again during the course of their lives. This may not have been Martin's first."

"Maybe that could be said for the rest of us," Dorothy contributed. "How do we know we haven't been abducted in the past?"

"This is getting too weird for me," said Jean. "I don't want to go anywhere. Stonecliff is good enough for me, even with its drawbacks."

"We may be making too much of this," said John. "What happened to Martin may have nothing to do with the rest of us. We're going too far out with this speculation."

"Well, like Jean said, we couldn't pass the physical," said Dorothy. "Although I'm still for going to that cave and trying out the waters. It can't hurt to try."

"Is that your 'will' speaking or an insidious thought place in your mind by these aliens," Laura smiled.

"God! What is this doing to all of us that we question every thought or move as being programmed by aliens," Dorothy exclaimed.

"It is something to think about," Jeff said. "Are we going to have to put everyone under hypnosis in order to find what's human or alien?"

"What now?" Martin asked.

"Well, we started this mostly out of curiosity," said Jim, "because Martin disappeared for two years. Now we know--or think we know. It's possible we may be in danger from these aliens. They don't seem to do physical harm, but they would seem to disrupt lives."

"And yet, what can we do to protect ourselves," Jeff added. "These aliens have the power to do what they wish. Furthermore, they come at a time when you're most vulnerable--when you're asleep. And locked doors and windows can't stop them."

"Not when they walk through cave walls," Martin agreed.

"So, what do we do if we're going to take this seriously?" John asked.

"Nothing much," said Jeff. "Unless everyone wants to sleep together at the gym. Even that is no guarantee."

"Are we the only ones involved?" asked Dorothy. "What about the rest of the class? Are they in the same fix as we are and if so, shouldn't we tell them? They have a right to know."

"Know what?" Jeff asked. "Right now we don't know if what we know is any good or not. We don't have enough evidence to present to them to back up our suspicions."

"Then we'll get it," Martin spoke up. "The reservation is my home, what's left of it. I'll go back there, build a home and carry on as we were before the catastrophe. If the little people come again, then so be it. If someday you find me missing, then you'll know they took me again."

John nodded. "Very well, I'll go with you."

"What about me?" wailed Jean. I don't want to be stuck out there by myself, a target for God knows what. I lost a family once. Now this," she swung her arm, "is my family. Dorothy, Jim, the Umbralls, all the class is what I have left."

"Jean is right," said Martin. "All of you stick together. I'm not afraid of being alone. I was that before. Besides, if they take me again, I won't mind. I've seen this other world and it is beautiful.

"I'll need some help to start with. I've got to build a home and restock the cave. Something tells me I must do that."

"A thought implanted in your mind," smiled Laura.

"It could be," Martin smiled in return.

"I'll get construction material from Aaron," said John.

"There's no need of anyone going by themselves," said Jim. "We can go in groups like we did last time. We'll take turns. I think we should update the Umbralls and the Bonococcis. They were there when Martin appeared so they know something's up. We should also start getting some of the others aware of our suspicions regardless of whether or not they want to believe. To start with, I would include the Sherlands, the Granhills, the Wadleys and I think Laura should let Walter know what we've been doing here. This way, if there are any strange disappearances, those remaining won't be in ignorance of what happened.

"Are we in agreement?"

"Yes, I agree," said Jeff. "But if Martin will have me, I'll move out there with him. I don't have any family here to be missed."

"Why do you want to put yourself in possible danger," Laura asked. "It makes no sense."

"Am I? I don't know that I am. My knowledge on the subject is that people have been abducted with a companion sitting next to them or picked up from a group of people in a public place. So it can happen wherever you are or with whom you are."

"Very well," she tossed her hair. "It's your life I suppose. You have a right, among others, of doing stupid things."

"Yes. Lucky for me, our right wing politicians haven't passed a constitutional amendment forbidding that. They would be the first ones indicted."

"But you're our only expert on this--this..."

"Paranormal is the word most often used."

"Whatever. So why isolate yourself in the boondocks."

"You forget. Our main subject will be out there. I will

be with him."

"Then go. I won't stop you."

"No you can't. But feel free to drop in once in a while."

"I may have to. You need a doctor to sign the death certificate."

"Yes, well. Trouble is, there may not be a body to certify."

"The session is over," she turned away and went out the door.

"You think she's really concerned for me?" Jeff turned to Dorothy.

"I think she is. But don't push it. You are on the verge of controlling the situation, whatever that is. But the lady is not one to lose control."

CHAPTER SIXTEEN

Two days later a group was gathered at the schoolhouse. Jim had called the meeting and along with the Fenzers. The Eddlemans, Jeff, Laura and Martin, he had called in the Sherlands, the Granhills, the Umbralls, the Bonococcis and Walter Heerlson and his two nurses, Ellen Service and Stella Mundick. There were twenty people altogether.

"Everyone knows each other, but I don't think all of you know Martin Hill who is the shaman of John's tribe. He has, or rather, we found a startling story concerning him that may or may not concern us.

"A group of us made a trip to this cave in John's reservation. The Umbralls and the Bonococcis went with us. We invited several of you, but you didn't show up, although I remember that Tom and Jane made a trip out there two years ago with the Eddlemans, the Kendalls and the Jabotys.

He told them what had occurred at the cave site and how Martin had appeared, scaring Sylvia and having no memory that two years had elapsed.

"Sylvia scared out of her pants?" Linda Sherland laughed. "How could I have missed that? After all the misery she has heaped on us that would have been sweet payback."

"Go ahead and laugh," Sylvia glowered. "I'd like to see you go in there."

"I will, honey, if you lead the way."

Jim rapped the table with his knuckles. "Let's hold off on the fun and games until we finish this.

"As it is, it might pay for all of us to go in that cave, but I'll let Dr. Criden explain that later. Let me finish the story on Martin." He explained the recent session Laura had with Martin, his abduction, his stay in a strange land and then his return after two years.

"Look," said Aaron. I don't know why you're telling us this. I don't want to insult anyone's intelligence, but these kind of stories have been floating around for as long as I can remember. And you're right, I don't know Martin, but as deference to John, I'll withhold judgment."

"That's all I ask," said Martin. "And in the end, all this may not have anything to do with any of you. It's only that John and I have encountered these creatures, so maybe it's an Indian thing. Then again, maybe it's not, but we should be aware in case it does affect anyone else."

"Let me step in here with some hard evidence," Jeff spoke up. "During Martin's session with Dr. Criden, it was brought out that other people had been abducted, two of them at the same time as Martin. These people were the Toland family from Ohio and the Anders from Kansas. The Tolamd's told Martin it was 2019 when they were taken. The Anders disappearance was the same year as Martin's, 2020.

"Using my position as the congressmen's aide, I asked for lists of missing persons in the respective states. I got the list yesterday. No one else has seen them except for Dr. Criden and me.

"Since Jim had already mentioned getting more of you involved, I asked him if he could call you people today. Because Laura and I went over the lists and yesterday and those two families were listed as missing for the two years of 2019 and 2020!"

There was stunned silence.

"To me, that's the first clear evidence that those tales of alien abductors are not somebody's nightmare or hallucinations brought by an overdose of drugs." Jeff continued.

"All right. Assuming that everything that happened to Martin is true, how does this affect the rest of us?" Aaron asked.

"Possibly none at all," replied Jeff. "We're just trying to touch all bases. However, consider this, why was Martin returned and not the others? Why were we able to get all the information from him when many other abductees have a loss of memory that even hypnosis cannot bring out? Is it possible aliens are trying to condition us by letting out Martin's experiences. That there is a good and beautiful world somewhere that lacks only colonists?"

Aaron snorted. "Now you're way out, Jeff. But go ahead and put it in writing. Hollywood might buy it."

Jeff nodded. "O.K. We've heard your views. Anyone else have something to say?"

Laura broke in. "Let me say my piece, Jeff, and then you can have a vote or whatever it is that Jim was planning for this meeting.

"As all of you know, it was determined through tests that all of you are sterile except two. For those of you who know, Jim and John are those two. And to that short list we can add Martin."

"This is the ultimate in machismo," said Sylvia. "All three are male."

"I doubt that is the common factor," Laura continued. "If so, several more males would have qualified.

"No, the common factor in all three is that they spent a considerable amount of time at the cave."

"Are you saying that these aliens immunized all three against--whatever it was that affected the rest of us?" Aaron spoke up.

"No, I'm not saying that, but that is a thought we hadn't considered.

"What I had in mind were the waters found inside the

cave. All three men drank and bathed in that water for several months. I've sent a sample of the water to Atlanta.

"Dorothy and Jim are convinced that the water might help them. However, if there is any magical power in that water, it might take several months, just as it did with Jim and John, before we see any improvement."

"And that brings us back to this abduction problem," Jeff took over. "We're going to test the possibility that the water can help in this sterility problem. Which means that some or all of you might want to go there and try it.

"Oh, we can bottle some of it and bring it to Stonecliff, but we don't know if just drinking it is enough. Maybe it's the immersion that does the job.

"So if we're going to have excursions going there, we should also be prepared for the possibility these creatures might appear."

"One last thing," said Jim. "As far as we know, there is no protection from these abductors. These beings have incredible power. If they want you, there's not much you can do about it. They invaded John's house here in Stonecliff even though all doors and windows were locked. And they took Martin from the cave.

"So if there are any strange disappearances of any of us, we will know what happened. Not that it will do us any good. We have no defense against them."

"Well, that's just great," said Tom. "How did the rest of us get involved in this?"

"As we said before, you may not be. And they may be only after a select number of us," Jim replied.

"Martin and I are going out there tomorrow or the day after," John said. "Aaron, I'd like to get some building material and also look into setting up some sort of communication between here and there. The tribe will pay for everything."

Aaron nodded. "Don't worry about payment. If that cave of yours can cure Linda and me, that's payment enough."

"Nancy and I want to go along," said David. "We'll pitch in."

"No problem, Dave," said John. "Great to have you. It will be like the old days on the River Road,"

"Well, hell," said Tom. "Count me and Jane on that trip."

"Day after tomorrow is Friday," said Jim. "Anyone wanting to go, show up by seven in the morning at the supermarket parking lot. Wear your casual clothes, it's going to be a working weekend,"

"Want to go, honey?" Oscar asked Esther.

"Sure, why not."

"You're going to leave me alone?" wailed Sylvia.

"No, Carl will be here," said Esther.

"Carl won't be here." said Carl. "I'm going to try the waters. You should too, Sylvia."

"I'm too young to be a mother."

"We're all too old to be childless couples," said Linda.

CHAPTER SEVENTEEN

Everyone at the meeting turned up Friday morning except Ellen Service who had a weekend shift at the hospital. Jim was elated at the turnout.

"I don't want to sound cynical," said Dorothy, "but do you reckon the idea those waters might solve their sterility problem have anything to do with it?"

He shrugged. "It doesn't matter. I want them out there so they might get a better grasp on a potential problem."

The caravan consisted of five vans and a trailer carrying the building materials. There were few people about at that time of the morning so they didn't attract much attention.

"I feel guilty for not asking the others in the class if they wanted to participate," said Jim. He and Dorothy and the Edlemans were alone in one van.

"In hindsight, I agree with you," said Dorothy. "But there's still several of the women who have no mates. They might feel uncomfortable."

"We should have asked George and Thelma," said

John.

"After all, Thelma is one of the Chosen, according to Martin." Jim shook his head. "Sometimes it's hard to keep everything in perspective. Is Martin's world just a fantasy he made up? And if it isn't, how are we involved? He still seems to be pushing that 'Chosen' fable."

"You're not going to convince that crowd with that angle," said Dorothy. "Aaron, for one, is a hard-headed business man. The only reason he's going is because of the possibilities of that water. He and Linda want an heir."

"There's probably more that think like Aaron," said Jean. "And you can't blame them. They've gone through one horrible experience. Two in one lifetime is too much."

They arrived at the cave shortly before eleven. Immediately the newcomers wanted to see the pool. So everyone trooped in and everyone had to drink the water.

Jim finally led them outside. "How about the ladies fix up lunch while the guys unload the trailer."

The rest of the day went by quickly and by late afternoon, the cabin foundation was finished. The women had barbecue ready. The men took a dip in the pool, followed by the women. Then they sat down for the evening meal at sundown.

"This will make a nice vacation retreat," said Aaron.

"Especially when the trees grow up again."

"Yes, the tribe needs to get back in business," said Martin.

"All two of us," added John.

"Well, we could make all these folks honorary Indians," said Martin. "Do you reckon the U.S. government would recognize honorary?"

"Yeah," said Sylvia. "Just like an honorary degree makes you smarter."

"Does anyone feel any different?" Laura asked. "You had a dip in the pool and drank water like it was going out of style." Laura had ridden in Jeff's van along with Walter and Stella as she had briefed the latter two on her experience with Martin.

"I feel bloated enough to think I'm already pregnant,"

said Esther.

"If what you suspect is true," said Walter, "I doubt there will be any reactions this soon."

"You've heard Laura's story," said Dorothy. "What's your opinion, Walter?"

"Incredible. Hard to believe. But you can't dismiss it. Every day medical science is coming up with cures for some of our worse diseases. Our South American forests, what's left of them, have given us uncountable sources of new medicines. And the human mind, huh, there's so much to learn about it. I don't know what to tell you. It's a waiting game. What's impossible today, may be possible tomorrow."

"What a copout, Walter," said Sylvia.

"Listen to her," said Oscar. "That, from a woman who lives her life by a TV schedule."

"Go hug a tree!" snapped Sylvia.

"Can't--Your dog's using it."

"Personally, I think there's a good possibility Sylvia was abducted a long time ago," said Esther.

"Yeah--and rejected," said Oscar.

"That is a thought," said Laura. "Do any of you have any recollection of lost time or a strange inexplicable events?"

"Oh, no! You're not serious about that, are you?" Aaron looked askance.

She shrugged. "What's wrong with asking? You don't have to considered it if you don't want to. But if anyone has, it would be interesting in view of what's happened."

"It happened to one man--or he thinks it did," said Aaron.

"Right. And if anyone else went through the same experience, it becomes less rare," she replied.

"That's the keyword--rare," said Jeff. "And the paranormal is not rare. There's any number of books written on the subject. Some are hoaxes no doubt.

"People disappearing? There's several stories of people who did disappear like Martin, though no one is on record of having been gone for two years.

"There's instances of people who suddenly find

themselves transported thousands of miles away. There was probably some lost time there.

"UFO sightings? By now there must be tens of millions who have seen them. Probably more than that have failed to report them because they were afraid of public ridicule.

"Here in Arizona and New Mexico, seems to be a hot spot for sightings. Indeed, most of the stories of UFO crashes and recovery of ships and aliens have come from these two states."

"Oh, great!" exclaimed Sylvia. "Gather around the campfire, girls. Let's see who can tell the scariest ghost story."

"Oh, I don't know," said Jeff. "It's not scary. It's fascinating trying to discover all the mysteries of life. Who are we? Why are we here? What's our purpose in life? Where are we going? Is there life after this?"

"Whoa, Jean Dixon," replied Sylvia. "You're off on another esoteric binge. Jim and Carl are the ones that like to get into those questions."

Jim smiled. "You're not the first one to ask those questions. And it's hard to get answers because our past has been filled with so much garbage.

"For all those hoaxes of the paranormal, there are just as many, if not more, in our so-called normal world. We don't know where we're going because we don't know who we are and where we've been.

"American history is laden with myth and legend trans-formed into fact. We need heroes, so we manufacture them. We need bogey men, so we heap scorn on a few detestable creatures in order to contrast with our goodness. We tell our friends, be like us, a democracy, but we don't follow our words with deeds in our own country and our own citizens.

"Our monuments, statues and public buildings have high sounding phrases engraved in concrete which belie the actual practice."

"Your soapbox is teetering," said Sylvia.

Jim grunted. "We're telling scary stories, remember?

Everything I just said should be scary."

"When the world ends, we'll fix it for the next go-around," said Dorothy.

"When will that be?" Jim asked. "We just slipped into a new century which many predicted we would never live to see. 1999, 2000. All those nines and zeros seemed to fascinate those prophets that said those were the Ends of our time.

“But here we are in 2022. The only accident that could have ended our world was local and man-made. Although in the End, it will probably be a man-made or series of man-made incidents that will contribute to the End.

"You see, prophets have been making these predictions since people came into this world. The same dire predictions made for the year 2000, they made for the year 1000--and several for years in-between. There was--is, no pattern for these warnings.

“Every little disturbances from normal was the forerunner of the Big Event. Every person that attained a little notoriety became the Antichrist or the new Messiah. But the Time came and went and when nothing happened, a new date was forecast and new players cast as the main characters. Pick a name out of your history books and at some time in the past someone had identified it as the Antichrist or the Messiah."

"The world ends for each of us when we die," said Jeff. "How more final can you get?"

"Exactly," said Jim. "We try to plan our future for our immediate lifetime and that of our children and grandchildren. That's why most of you came here. Not because you believe in UFOs or alien abduction. That's crazy, you say. But gee, isn't there a possibility that the water in that cave can cure our problem? That's not crazy at all?"

"All right, Jim," laughed Aaron. "I get your point."

It was already dark. They threw more wood into the fire. The women cleaned up while the men prepared the sleeping arrangements.

"We'll put Sylvia's stuff in her van," said Oscar. "She's very hostile towards the reptile species."

"Don't start that crap again, Oscar," Sylvia snarled.

"I owe you for the last one. Do you want to run up the score?"

"I'm not so worried about snakes as I am about bats," said Jane Wadley. "Are there any in that cave?"

"Only in your belfry," said Sylvia. "God, Jane, I've got enough problems with snakes, now I have to worry about bats?"

"We've got some mosquito netting," said Dorothy. "Just put it over you. That way the bats get tangled in the netting instead of your hair."

"Show some sympathy for a member of your gender," Sylvia glared. "Ever since you got married, you've forgotten your old friends of the female variety."

"Yes, and if memory serves, my female friends are also married. 'Woman should cleave unto her husband.' So sayeth the Bible."

"Quote me no quotes from the Bible," Sylvia chortled.

"For every quote you can come up, I'll match with one that is completely the opposite."

"The applicability of Biblical lore to modern life is like saying we should live our lives as they were when the Constitution was written," grinned Jeff.

The group was laying out their sleeping bags around the fire. All but five of the nineteen were married couples.

The exceptions being Martin, Jeff, Laura, Walter and Stella. Consequently there was care in the positioning of sleeping bags belonging to the singles. "Who turned on the light?" complained Sylvia, as the campfire scene was suddenly brightened.

"Oh, God! Look!" Linda screamed, pointing upwards.

The night sky was obscured by a huge disc-shaped ship. The lights on its perimeter changed colors as it whirled around like a giant merry-go-round. Only a faint humming sound could be heard from the vehicle. As it circled over the group, a hatch opened from its dark underbelly and a beam of bluish light streamed down a few yards away from the awed spectators.

"You have to believe me now," Martin croaked.

CHAPTER EIGHTEEN

It was the typical gray-green government office that was so common a couple of decades ago--and the present occupants preferred it that way, refusing modernization. The office was medium size, two desks, swivel chairs, filing cabinets, a couch and two sitting chairs not designed to provide comfort to the occasional visitor--and occasional was an overstatement.

There was a man looking out the lone window at a skyline that anyone would instantly recognize as belonging in the nation's capital. Actually the window faced out the rear of the building, but the familiar skyline was visible because the building in back was only two stories high.

The second man was sitting at his desk reading a memo which he slammed down on the desk. "Another bunch of sightings out West," he grunted. "And guess what? They want us to check it out."

"Where out West?"

"Arizona."

"Close. If it's not Arizona, it's New Mexico.

"What's so particular about these sightings that we have to check them out in person? And that we haven't already heard a thousand times before?"

"For one thing, it's in the area that was wiped out two years ago with that new atmospheric weapon."

"So? What does the Great Analyst think is going on out there? That the Martians are checking out the effects of the weapon? If so, why now? It happened two years ago."

"Maybe it took them two years of space travel to get here," sarcastically. "How the hell would I know?"

"Look, Mitch, I don't think it worth going out there for something we've gone over a dozen times. So what if it's over that devastated area in Arizona. We've had sightings over our most classified areas and we've found zilch. Why should this be different?"

"For one thing, it's orders from the Great Analyst, as you call him..."

"As everyone else calls him."

"Whatever. And second, if you let me finish, there's been a request for Missing Person's List from Ohio and Kansas."

"Again, so what."

"Our computer nerds down in the basement keep track of such things. Every abduction or suspected abduction is in that computer by state, by year and with all the necessary description of the victims. It seems that just recently a request was made to acquire those lists for those two states for the years 2019 and 2020, respectively."

"Mitch, I hate repeating myself, but what has that got to do with the sightings?"

"Maybe nothing. But the request came from a Jeff Randall, an aide to Congressman Sawyer from Arizona. Randall is out there liaising for the congressman."

"Maybe they found some bodies or identification tying in to someone in those states? Perfectly normal for them to ask for missing person's list to confirm the person was missing before they go off half-cocked and upset their family."

"Right. And maybe that's all there is to it."

"All right. Let me use all my investigative powers on this one. There's reports of UFO sightings over Arizona. The same state that was devastated two years ago. Now there's a congressman's aide there asking for lists of missing persons for the years 2019 and 2020 for two different states hundreds of miles away from Arizona.

"Now tell me how you can connect all these facts to make any sense, Mitch?"

"That must be why the Great One wants us out there to find out." Mitch got up and walked to the window. He was short, about five seven, but trim, about a hundred thirty five pounds, moonface, somewhere in his fifties. The man at the window was just under six feet, well-built, a craggy face, topped off by a full head of black hair. He was about ten years younger than the other man.

"Jensen, we've been partners for almost ten years. We've investigated an untold number of cases for this outfit..."

"Yeah, right. Some investigations. Those so-called investigations consisted of scaring and intimidating the witnesses. Telling them they've seen something other than UFOs."

"That's our job and we have our orders."

"It's a shitty thing, Mitch. Either those things are real or they are a secret weapon."

"That's right. That's all we're supposed to deal with. If they are ours, then it's classified and nobody's business. If it's the real thing, then we don't want to cause panic by having some nut claiming an alien invasion."

"Yeah. Only it's not that simple, is it? You left out what happens when they don't cooperate. They disappear, don't they? Or just happen to have a fatal accident. Maybe that's what happened to those persons they're looking for on those missing person lists."

Mitch sighed. "It's all in our job description. Don't get self-righteous now. The time for backing out is way past."

"Those job descriptions don't tell all we have to do. Paper trail, you know. And do you think they would let us go after telling us what they wanted us to do?"

Mitch shrugged. "It's immaterial now."

"No, it isn't. If we ever want to leave, they're going to make certain we don't decide to write a book about it."

"Are you, Jensen?"

"No. Just thinking."

"Well don't. Thinking could be injurious to your health."

"You, Mitch?"

“That’s something we don’t have to worry about, do we?”

CHAPTER NINETEEN

The next two weeks after the sightings saw hurried activity at the cave site. The cabin was completed, large enough to hold the expected visitors to the cave pool. Martin, in the meantime, made an inventory of his supplies at the cave. He threw away what was out-of-date and started to restock with new and fresh supplies.

John was skeptical of the latter move. It was a waste of money, not to mention the spoilage of food.

"Just go along with me on this, John."

"Martin, right now we're all right financially. We're even earning some interest on our accounts. But there's nothing coming in from our former businesses. I've contacted someone to clear two of our lakes so we can resume fishing. Of course, we need to restock. But the skiing and ranching will take longer--if ever."

"Don't worry about it, John. After we finish here at this site. We'll see what we can do about the rest."

"I--we, will have to come up with something. The government made a generous settlement with Jean and me, but it won't last forever. I haven't had to draw any money from the tribal account except for tribal business, which is nil at this time. Unless we do something out of this land, we'll probably have to abandon it and get a job somewhere else."

"Trust me, John. We'll make out." And that was the best John could get out of him.

The whole class now knew about the pool in the cave and its potential miracles. Consequently, there was always a large group around to help Martin and John with their labors.

The episode with the UFO had made believers out of the onlookers that night. No one could offer a plausible explanation so they were forced to believe it was what it was--a UFO, a spaceship. But certainly not a weather balloon, swamp gas or the Planet Venus.

It had stopped overhead but not directly over them. When the bluish beam of light came down, it was off to the side of the group. They had gotten a clear look at the vehicle, then it had slowly moved a few yards away. There it hovered for a few minutes. Then the onlookers saw a large tree that had fallen to the ground during the late disaster suddenly being lifted into the ship, apparently using the blue light as the lifting source. The tree must have weighed several hundred pounds, but it was lifted easily, though slowly towards the open hatch on the ship's belly.

Then suddenly, the light flicked off and the tree crashed to the ground. The humming sound grew louder, the swirling perimeter lights started changing colors and the outer rim of the ship accelerated, and the ship ascended. Then it took off at tremendous speed.

The group was left shaken and speechless. Not a few, particularly some of the women, were just plain scared. A guard detail was set up for the night. But even those excused from guard duty got any sleep that night.

Naturally, the next day generated heavy discussions on the subject. "At least no one can claim they've never seen a UFO," said Martin.

"I could have gone the rest of my life making that claim," said Sylvia.

"And we're all here," said Jeff. "No one got

abducted."

"Did anyone get the impression they were trying to tell us something?" Jim looked around for comments.

"I don't recall a heavenly voice coming from above," said Dorothy.

"Charlton Heston, maybe?" said Esther.

"Naw," said Sylvia. "He pushes guns now and I didn't hear no bang, bang."

"Did you get that impression?" Laura asked.

"Well, consider. It hovered over us, then moved to the side, opened its hatch and we saw the blue light."

"A K-Mart blue light special," cracked Sylvia.

Jim ignored her and continued. "Then we saw the tree being lifted through the light. Then just as suddenly, it was released and the ship took off."

"And what kind of message does that convey to you?" from Laura.

"Why show themselves to us when they're usually very secretive? Then it moves away from us before beaming down that light."

"Beam me up, Scotty." Sylvia exclaimed.

Jim glared at her. "This light apparently has the power or energy to levitate objects, but they made certain it wouldn't pick us up."

"An anti-gravity device?" Carl gave his opinion.

"That's as good a guess as any," Jim replied. "But the point I wanted to make is that they proceeded to lift up that tree, then dropped it and took off.

"Why pick up a tree when there's thousands laying on the ground and have been for the last two years. And if they really wanted that tree, why pick it up at that particular time and place? And then drop it?"

"Maybe it just slipped," said Aaron.

"From all we've seen or heard, they're pretty efficient," Jim shook his head. "No, I think their message was: Look, we're here. We're not some sorry excuse put out by your government. We can pick you up just like we can pick up this tree. Don't be afraid of us."

"Wow!" Sylvia exclaimed. "You got all that in one

moment of silence while we were all wetting our underpants?"

"So that was you I smelled," grinned Oscar.

"These people don't say much," Martin contributed, "but somehow they get their message across."

"You agree with Jim?" John asked.

Martin shrugged. "It's a good premise. These aliens have their agenda and they're very single-minded in pursuing it."

"And what is that agenda?" Aaron asked.

"I can only tell you what Dr. Criden brought out in her examination. That one of their reasons for abducting humans is to settle and populate some distant planet. Whether that is all or only part of their agenda, I can't tell you."

"And why do that?" persisted Aaron.

"Maybe I can give you some reasons for that," said Jeff. "I can't vouch for the truthfulness of these accounts. Dozens of stories have been written and published by people who claim to have talked to these aliens. The story is that we are destroying our planet. They warn us of our nuclear excesses. And, of course, we have our own people warning us of the consequences if we ignore our environmental problems."

"You are right about that last part." said Aaron. "Business is the bogeyman who doesn't care how we treat the land, the air, our waterways, what we eat and where we build."

"Yes, well, anyway," Jeff continued, "There's been a common and constant thread in these stories of people talking to aliens. Supposedly they are alarmed, as I said, about our destroying the planet. Why, I don't know and these stories never make it clear why they are concerned. Maybe it will destroy some form of order in the galaxy. Perhaps these beings are not alien to our planet but reside here unseen or in another dimension. It could even be that they have genuine concern for the human race."

"I'm going to call your mother, Jeff, and have her throw away all those science fiction magazines in your closet," said Sylvia.

"Too late." smiled Jeff. "I came out of the closet many years ago.

"But seriously, we've heard of Martin's experiences. The time he spent on this unknown planet and at least two other families which we have identified as having once been inhabitants of this country.

"Could it be they know of some approaching catastrophe that will affect this planet? Is that why these two families were transported to a safe place and provided with all the essentials to make life bearable?"

"For once I agree with Sylvia," said Aaron. "You're going off half-cocked on this theory, Jeff. What you are suggesting sounds like one of these cults that periodically predict the end of the world. They get rid of all their belongings and travel to the top of some mountain to be picked up."

"There is a difference," replied Jeff. "There is no cult here. No one is disposing their property. Everyone here is free to believe or disbelieve. To go their own way."

"Has anyone thought that the one thing that has drawn us together is the sterility problem?" Dorothy remarked. "Martin's story alone would not have sufficed. It's too outrageous to believe. But we are willing to believe that the waters in that cave could solve our problem."

"That is something to ponder," said Jeff. "But don't forget they have the power to do anything they want with us at any time and at any place."

It was left at that. They finished their work on Martin's cabin that weekend.

In the days to follow they added extra touches. They set up a communication system between the cabin and Stonecliff. Around the cave site were set motion detectors and lights that could come on or off automatically or controlled by someone in the cabin. For that purpose a control panel was set in the cabin for the alarms and communication devices. A generator and back-up were installed.

"We're all set," said Martin when they had finished.

"Maybe," said Jim. "Somehow, I don't think all this will deter the aliens if they really want to get you. I seem to remember reading they turn off sources of power and energy."

"Then we'll be just as much in the dark as ever," smiled Martin.

CHAPTER TWENTY

The road was dark, pitch black, actually. The only light came from the sedan crunching on the gravel road at forty miles an hour.

"We're almost there," said Mitch. "I checked the odometer yesterday. It's only five miles away."

"There's nobody on the road," said Jensen. "If they don't see us coming, they'll surely hear us."

"They're about three miles in from the road. And this road ends about a few yards from where they go in. After that it's only a trail accessible only by a four-wheel drive, off-road vehicle. We'll leave the car at that point and walk in from there."

"Into what?"

"I don't know. I couldn't go anywhere from the road in broad daylight."

"Great! So we don't know what we're getting into."

"It won't be the first time."

"I got a feeling we won't get much from these people."

Jensen was gloomy. "Nobody back there had much to say."

"That's all right. All they could tell us was about the sightings. There's not much they can do with that. We're supposed to be couple of UFO nuts which means they will think we're crazy. But they did say there was a rumor of an abduction out here."

"Whatta we're going to do? Warn them not to be abducted?"

"All I want to know is what happened and have them keep their mouths shut."

"One of the construction workers said there has been a lot of traffic on this road recently. Sure don't look like it."

"Not likely anyone will be traveling at night," said Mitch. He slowed the car and turned off the lights.

"Damn!" Jensen exclaimed. "Can't see a thing."

"It's all right. We just passed my marker." The car stopped.

"You got everything we need?" Mitch turned to Jensen.

"We'll use our penlights, nothing else. We get out of the car quickly so the dome light won't stay on for long. Don't slam the door. Noise carries a long way out here. Ready?"

Jensen nodded, then realized Mitchell couldn't see him.

"Yeah."

"Go!"

They slid out and closed the doors softly. Jensen looked back into the car and saw a warning light on the instrument panel.

"Warning lights on. Door's not completely closed."

"Shove it with your ass! That's all we need, to come back to a car with a dead battery."

Jensen did so. There was a click and the light went off.

"Follow me," said Mitch. "There's tire tracks close by. We'll follow them."

"Is that wise? They could have an alarm set up."

"Yeah, they dug a pit with spikes at the bottom," Mitch was sarcastic. "Any other way means climbing over dead trees and dry brush. They'll hear us coming and with our luck we'd break a leg."

They picked their way carefully, briefly using their penlights. Vehicles had pressed down on the brush and flattened the trail which made their passage easier and without creating noise.

"How far are they?" whispered Jensen. "It's must be at least an hour since we left the road."

"I don't know. These tracks must end somewhere."

"Yeah, but how far? It's going to play hell if we have to make a quick exit."

Then, suddenly, lights came on. On each side of the road were poles set back and lights on each pole. In front of them, two lights shone straight into their eyes, blinding them.

"Please step forward," a voice commanded. "So you can see us."

They did so. Mitch cursing softly. They had been caught like rank amateurs.

They saw a large rustic cabin with a porch upon which were two men looking down on them. The one on the left was dressed in khaki shirt and trousers, boots and a bomber jacket. The one on the right had jeans, plaid flannel shirt and also sported boots. Both men were tall and well-built.

All this in contrast with their visitor's dark business suits.

"Welcome, gentlemen," the mean on the left spoke up.

"If you had told us you were coming, we would have had the lights on. That's a nasty walk from the road in the dark. "Would you care to come up and sit down?" he continued.

There were several chairs on the porch.

"Who are you?" Mitch blurted out."

"I believe that's my question since you're here uninvited and on private land."

"We're from the government," said Mitch.

"That's nice," said the man on the right. "So am I. At least Uncle Sam pays my salary. But we're not in the bootlegging business, if that's what you're looking for."

"We're not looking for bootleggers. Someone out here is spreading stories of UFO sightings and abductions. You know anything about that?"

"You say you're from the government?" from the man on the left. "That can't be. The government says there's no such thing as UFOs. So you're lying to us. They wouldn't send anyone out here to investigate something they say doesn't exist.

"Who do you represent? Let's see. The FBI is only supposed to be involved in domestic affairs. The CIA is only involved in..."

The man on the right snorted. "Let's get real, Jim.

“There may be laws and regulations set in concrete, but for some government agencies, they're written in disappearing ink. Every director of some tin-pot agency has his own security or intelligence outfit. Funding of which is hidden under Miscellaneous or some such account. After a while these 'intelligence' outfits start making their own rules and personal justification for their actions. And accountable to no one. They play James Bond and believe they have a 'license to kill.' Right, fellows? I bet these two bozos won't tell you the name of their agency."

"You seem to think you have all the answers," said Mitch.

"Oh, what a great comeback. Way to go, fellows. It still doesn't tell us who you really are.

"As for having all the answers, until two years ago I worked in that Tinsel Town of inflated egos and shear hypocrisy. Think of any rotten adjective and it helps describe that town."

"So, you think we're 'James Bond' types? Then if you think that, you should be careful what you say. Loose mouths cause panic."

"And that really pisses your bosses--whomever they are--and for whatever reason," said Jim.

"My friend, Mr. Randall, here, knows more of how

Washington works," continued Jim. "But I know my way around the boondocks. I make my living in out-of-the-way places like this.

"I suspect that underneath those coats you're carrying lethal weapons, which I'm sure you're experts in their use. You might even be able to draw them out and get my friend and me. But, you don't know everything, do you? Just like you didn't know about the lights. You didn't do your homework. You screwed up.

"Right now you see two men standing in front of you. But do you know if there's anyone else out there beyond these lights? You could have a rifle centered on your backs right now. You don't know if there's anyone else in that cabin.

"We've known you were here since you stopped your car on that road. We knew you were casing us since you first came down that road yesterday. We've known you were asking questions in Stonecliff. So we were expecting you.

"If these lights go out, do you think you could make it back to your car? And if you do, do you think you can get away from there?"

"Are you threatening agents of the U.S. government?"

Jeff laughed. "That takes the cake. You made the first threat. Now you're complaining because the tables were turned because of your stupidity.

"As for being agents of the government, well, talk is cheap. Show us some legitimate credentials."

The two visitors didn't answer or move to take him up on his request.

"The next step is up to you." said Jim. "You can back up your threat and pull your weapons. Or you can back up--all the way to your car. All the way back to Washington, or wherever you came from. We'll keep the lights on till you get to your car.

"Oh, and tell your bosses we're all honest and level-headed Americans. We don't panic. We've just proved that to you. The only panic seems to come from your bosses who don't trust the American people."

"We'll go," said Mitch. "But you haven't heard the last of this."

"You keep whistling that tune all the way to your car," said Jeff. "Because this better be the last we hear of this and this is the last we'll see of each other under such amiable circumstances."

Mitch and Jensen turned away, taking the clearly defined tire tracks towards the main gravel road.

"Did he bluff us?" Jensen asked.

"What do you think?"

"I would have backed you if you had pulled your piece."

"Which 'piece' is that?" Mitch couldn't resist. He was still tense.

"Well, I didn't see or hear anything from inside that cabin and I don't think there's anybody out here. He bluffed us. Damn!"

"Maybe. But they had those lights available and they didn't turn them on until we got to their porch steps. Then they hit the switch and those lights are in our eyes, blinding us. Any six year old could have taken us out at that moment. Doesn't that tell you anything?"

"All right. What now? Do we have a Plan B?"

"We don't have a Plan B because we've never needed one."

"But, they just as much as told us to get out of town."

"Well, if you keep up with your Western melodrama, you know nobody ever leaves town because there would be no story if they did."

They got to the car and got in. Mitch put the key in the ignition, then hesitated. Jensen noticed.

"You think they might have wired it?"

"You just finished telling me there was no one out there in the brush--and those two couldn't have gotten ahead of us." He turned the key slowly as Jensen cringed.

The car started smoothly and tense stomachs relaxed.

"I ain't forgetting this," said Jensen.

Mitch turned on the lights and saw a piece of paper stuck under the windshield wiper. Jensen saw it too.

Mitch opened the door and reached for it. With the door still open and the dome light on, they read: HAVE A NICE LIFE--WHAT'S LEFT OF IT.

Behind them, the lights went off.

CHAPTER TWENTY ONE

Jim and Jeff went inside the cabin when they heard the car start. They turned off the lights. Dorothy and Jean looked at them, rifles at port position. "We were ready to smash the window panes with our rifles and send warning shots over their heads," said Dorothy.

"What a waste of good glass," said Jim. "It's easier to raise the window."

"Well, I thought such a gesture would be more dramatic."

The back door opened and John and Martin came in. "They're gone," said John.

"We hasten their departure," added Martin.

"What did you do?"

John explained about leaving a note on the windshield.

"I don't know," Jim shook his head. "We may have pushed them too far. We humiliated them and made them slink away with their tails between their legs. They won't forget it. And they're the kind that take extreme measures to correct their mistakes."

"What can they do? Shoot us?" Jean interjected. "Our own government?"

"Our govrnment was shooting my ancestors over a hundred years ago," said John.

"That same government was also shooting some of your ancestors along the Southwestern borders of this country."

"As I said," Jeff remarked, "there are some rogue agencies in our government who answer to no one.

"Oh, I know. Another conspiracy buff, you say. That's how they try to throw you off. They resort to ridicule. That's what happened to the UFO controversy. They call everyone nuts, gadflies and other unprintable names.

"As for conspiracy, remember it only takes two persons plotting to commit a crime for it to be called a conspiracy. Check Webster for the definition."

"That fits our two visitors, said Dorothy.

"All right, but I can't understand their curiosity," said Martin. "What have we done to deserve their attention?"

"There's some theories about that," said Jeff. "One is that our government knows who these aliens are and have already been in contact with them. And may have come to some sort of understanding with them. The opposite of that is that the government can't explain this phenomena and chooses ridicule because it has no answers. The chief culprit here could be the Air Force. Think how embarrassing this is, especially at budget time, when they would be forced to admit they don't know who is violating our air space. Even worse, they can't catch or shoot them down. It would be a good bet the Air Force would be at the forefront in any attempt to silence anyone who could prove them as liars."

"Government, like the human body, seems to have its own immune system, ready to fight any attempt of a foreign body or substance that invades the system," said Jim.

"So much for the political commentary," said Dorothy. "What do we do to protect ourselves?"

"We're pretty well set here," said Martin. "It would be difficult for them to sneak up on us."

"That's true," said John. "But now they have a better idea of our setup here."

"How far out is our defense perimeter?" Dorothy asked.

"Defense perimeter?" Jim grinned. "Well, General D. Fenzer, right now it extends about a hundred yards around the cabin except the road which extends all the way to the main road."

"Maybe we should extend it farther out, so they won't try to fire the cabin with flaming arrows," said Martin.

"And add some motion detectors--plus putting some on top the cliff in case they try rolling down boulders," added John.

"Gee. I'm glad you guys are up-to-date on modern warfare," laughed Jeff. "Expect the unexpected."

"John," Martin looked at him. "I think it's time we start tracking a couple of coyotes. No telling when they might return to snap at our heels."

Mitch and Jensen returned to their motel on the state highway west of Stonecliff.

"Shall we start preparing Plan B?" Jensen asked.

"Since you're so obsessed with this Plan B crap, suppose you tell me what we should do."

"Well, I've been thinking. We haven't seen or heard anything new on this UFO business that we haven't heard before. So why don't we just pack it up."

"That's your Plan B? This from a man who wanted to shoot it out? The guy who wasn't forgetting what happened to us? Hell, Jensen. We're acting like those Three Stooges."

"Don't we need another guy to qualify for that?"

"You think I'm trying to be funny? I couldn't be more serious. You forget we have to report back. What are we supposed to tell the Great One?"

"What's wrong with the truth?"

"That we got snookered? And by now you should

know that truth is something we don't always want to deal with."

"No--I mean, there's nothing out here to investigate."

"Oh? There isn't? Then why do they have all those lights around that cabin in the middle of nowhere? Why were they keeping tabs on us all along?"

"It's kinda lonely out there, I guess. Maybe all they're doing is protecting themselves."

"Against whom?--Or what?"

"Yeah, well--but do we care? Unless they're set up to protect themselves against UFOs."

"And how do you protect against UFOs? Anti-aircraft guns? Hell, the Air Force can't shoot them down. We know they can turn off power. So in my book there's nothing we can do to stop them. And then there's all this crap of alien abductions. If there's any truth to that, how do you stop it?"

"Yeah, I've read these books about how these aliens are supposed to abduct people. They pick them up anywhere, in singles, in groups, in the city, in the country. But how much of that is just bullshit, I don't know."

"I can't get it out of my mind that there's something out there that they're hiding. It don't make sense."

"Then we're back to what I said earlier. We don't have anything to investigate. If they have committed some crime or done something shady, then it's out of our jurisdiction."

"Ah, but we don't know that for sure."

"All right. But doesn't that put us back on Plan B?"

"Yeah, Jensen. It looks like you're gonna get your Plan B after all. Make you happy?"

"Don't matter one way or another as far as I'm concerned. We come up with a plan or get the hell out of here. So give me what you've got."

"Everybody's talking about abductions so why not give them one?" he looked sideways at Jensen.

"What do you mean?"

"Simple. We abduct one of these people and find out what's going on out there."

"Isn't that kidnapping?"

"Oh? Aren't you nitpicking? Nowadays the federal government does not distinguish between murder and kidnapping. The Lindbergh Law, remember?

"Besides, I prefer to call it 'alien abduction.' No one will know the difference."

"Alien abductees are returned to where they were picked up. They will know the difference--and tell."

"Don't be naive, Jensen. We couldn't afford to return them so they could tell."

Jensen's eyes widened, then he nodded. "I suppose our abductees would be one or both of those men at the cabin?"

"Yes, they would be the most likely candidates, but let's make it easier on ourselves. Let's pick on their women."

"That Jeff Randall is single. He's the one who came from Washington. So unless you want to go back there and look up his old girlfriends, that leaves us the other guy."

"Exactly. Let's find out more about Jim."

CHAPTER TWENTY TWO

Martin and John initiated their search for their erstwhile visitors. One of their stops was at the gas and automotive business now run by Frank Jaboty, a member of the surviving group.

After preliminary greetings, John asked him if he had seen two men, strangers, one shorter than the other, possibly wearing business suits and driving a dark, heavy car.

"Yeah, sure. I've seen them," said Frank. "They stood out, wearing those suits. No one around here wears suits unless they're going to a wedding or a funeral--or maybe one of those visiting government officials. Even the media types have learned to dress down if they expect the folks around here to feel comfortable with them."

"You have any idea where they came from? Where they're staying?"

He shook his head. "Not from around here. The two times I saw them I got the impression they drove in from that direction," pointing to the west.

"They could be staying in some motel on Highway 87."

"That's a good lead. We'll try looking there."

"What's the problem with these men?"

"We caught them sneaking up on the cabin the other night. They claim to be government agents, but they never flashed any credentials. Claim to be looking for people who had sighted UFOs."

"That again?" Frank laughed. "I wish I had a dollar for every UFO nut that has come by asking about them."

"These guys were armed and they made threats."

"Oh, then this is serious. Anything we can do to help? I know Anna was cheered at the possibility of the cave water helping our situation. I wouldn't want some outsiders coming in to ruin that."

"Yes, you can help. If you see them again, call me or Jim, Martin or Jeff, wherever we are, whatever the time. Get their license number, anything you overhear and in what direction they're going when they leave here."

"Can do. No problem. Keep me up-to-date on this, will you?

"And, by the way, if you find the car and want to keep it under surveillance, why not go over to Gil Borders' place and get a tracking device. Stick it under the chassis. You'll know where it is at all times--within limits, of course."

"I've heard of that. Seen it in the movies," said Martin.

John nodded. "That's a good idea. I'll make a stop at Gil's place."

Gilbert Borders was another of the survivors and a member of the Class of '05', as were all the survivors. So was his wife, the former Susan Gilbert. They had joked that if a husband had to take his wife's name, he would be known as Gilbert Gilbert.

The two men stopped at his place of business, an electronic store. After explaining the situation to him, he got the devices they needed and explained how to use them. They got two of the systems.

John and Martin drove out on the street leading to the state highway. Motels had sprung up on this street and on the highway to accommodate the influx of construction workers. So far, Stonecliff had only one modest hotel, which though moderate in price was not suited for long term occupancy.

"How are we going to do this?" Martin asked. "Do we go around each motel and ask if they have a couple of men that fit our description? How is that going to go over with these motel people, having a couple of Indians asking questions?"

"Yeah," John's mouth was grim. After all these years, you still couldn't change human nature. A new millennium had failed to change much. A man-made date was just that. A dividing line, when crossed, that didn't change things or people.

"Let's cruise around and see if we can spot the car before we try interviewing. It's almost four in the afternoon. Most workers are still on the job. Maybe these guys are in their room. If we can't find anything, we'll get Jim or Jeff to do the asking."

"It was a Buick, I'm sure," said Martin. "Four door, late model. I remember the grill design."

They drove west on the main street of Stonecliff, looking at several motels at the edge of town. Coming to the highway, they turned left that would lead them to Phoenix if they went far enough. But they had no luck in that direction.

"Most people out here, even tourists, drive vans or pickups. Any sedans are old and beat up," said John. "You won't see many big, heavy sedans out here."

"That's why it should be easy to spot," said Martin.

"Maybe they left."

"Not according to your friend, Frank Jaboty."

"Yeah, well, let's try the other direction and call it a day."

They turned back and drove past the street that went into Stonecliff.

"If they really came from Washington, it would make sense they would come in on I-40. It has been cleared now.

They would drive south and stop at one of these

motels north of the Stonecliff entrance," John speculated.

There wasn't much traffic on the highway, so they drove at a slower pace. Anyone seeing them would have taken them for what they were, a couple of Indians, native to the area, driving a pickup. On the interstate and connecting roads, this was a common sight.

At the second motel, they hit it--or at least it looked promising.

"Did you see that?" exclaimed Martin.

"Yeah, we need a closer look."

John continued on to the next motel where he made a turn. Driving as slowly as he dared on a highway, they took another look.

"It looks like it," said Martin. "I would be sure if I could see the grill."

"I saw a Coke machine near the office," said John. "Why don't you get down, get us a couple. That will give you a chance to look at the grill."

John returned for the third time, hoping they weren't conspicuous. He let Martin out a few yards from where the car was parked, giving the old man a chance to walk by the vehicle.

Martin walked on a narrow sidewalk, then stopped to light a cigarette a few feet away from the car. Then he continued slowly to the Coke machine. Then he returned the same way clutching his two cans of pop and got in the truck.

He was smiling. "That's the one. And what cinched it was a little piece of paper under the wiper. They must have jerked our note out and left the evidence behind. Good thing it hasn't rained.

"So what now?"

"It's much too early to do anything right now. It won't get dark until almost nine. So we'll attack at dawn like our forefathers."

“Great!” Martin slapped him on the back. “I like that.”

CHAPTER TWENTY THREE

"All right, Charlie. Is this all?"

"Ah, no, Mr. President. One more item of a minor nature and one which you took a personal interest."

"What matter are we talking about?"

Charles McNamara, the president's chief-of-staff and close friend, looked at his boss speculatively. It had been a long and frustrating day, mostly with the politics of obstruction. He wasn't sure his boss was in the mood for more problems.

"You remember our problem out West two years ago? The bomb gone awry?"

"Oh God! Don't remind me. I still don't know how I recovered from that. Is there a problem out there again?"

"You recovered because it wasn't your fault and you took steps to remedy the situation. It happened in the first six months of your administration on a problem initiated by your predecessors. And since then you've had time to make your own record."

"You didn't answer my question, Charlie. Do we have a problem out there?"

"You remember Jim Fenzer, the leader of the group that survived the whole mess? Well, he called me. The last time I saw him, two years ago, I told him to call me directly. I wanted to head off any future problems that might spring up there. We have a lot of government agencies out there, involved in cleaning and helping rebuild the area. It's a prime breeding ground for scams, fraud, chicanery and other mischief."

The President nodded. "I remember him. Independent, decisive. Too bad we don't have more like him."

"Yes, well, he called me yesterday. It seems there were two men out there calling themselves government agents, but never offered proof to that effect. They were caught sneaking in the dark around a cabin in the Indian reservation. They wanted to know about UFOs and alien abductions. Fenzer and his party chased them off, but they made threats and said something about this not being the end of it.

"Fenzer asked me if I knew of any intelligence agency involved or any covert activity being carried out in the vicinity."

"UFOs and alien abduction?"

"He was only repeating what the men told him. As far as paranormal tales are concerned, he said, it was normal out there to report sightings, and alien abduction stories are in the same category.

"Ordinarily I would be inclined to treat such stories as absurd. But coming from a fellow like Fenzer, I had second thoughts."

"So, why are you telling me this?"

"To prepare you in case a flap occurs. So you won't be caught unawares like the last time, two years ago.

"I called the FBI, the CIA and the NSA. I told them to send us any information on their activities out there. The reasons why, who authorized it and for what purpose."

"And? Do we have a reply?"

"No. Not that I expect any specific details to be released. But the request will make them aware that the White House has an interest on what happens out there. You appoint directors to these agencies, but they are never allowed to penetrate the deep layers of their bureaucracy."

"So, how should I remedy that?"

"The only way would be to fire the whole bunch and start over again. The trouble with that is that in a few years things would be back as they were before.

"The laughable part is that The Congress gives them blank checks and then when something goes wrong, you get it in the neck."

"Tell me something new.

"Well, keep me informed. I admire those people. What they did under the most stressful and horrible conditions. In fact, maybe I ought to make a trip back there to check how they are doing. It wouldn't hurt and it's definitely better than a speech before some chamber of commerce."

"I think that's a good idea. I'll check your schedule. If not now, then next year for sure. It should help your re-election campaign."

The man, tall, lanky, beautiful white hair and immaculately dressed in a three-piece suit, stood at the window and looked at the same skyline that could be seen from the office of Mitch and Jensen.

That was the only similarity. The office was several stories higher; it was larger; it was tastefully furnished.

The man walked back to his desk, an ornate affair, to answer a ringing telephone. Immediately he saw the call was from his boss on a private line.

"Yes?" as he picked it up.

"Stewart!" a voice bawled. "What are you up to?"

"I don't understand, sir," he grimaced at the tone of his superior. "What, specifically, am I accused of doing?"

"I just got a call from the Director, who got a call

from the Oval Office wanting explanations on our purported activities in Arizona."

"Well, 'purported' is the right word to use. We're not doing anything that we haven't done before, wherever we may have to go to conduct our investigations."

"That might be a good obfuscator reply to give our Director, but it's not good enough for me. The man is a political hack who will be gone in a couple of years. That's the way the system works and we have to put up with it. But from my level on down, we have to deal with reality and the imperfections of mankind. Trust no one."

"Sounds like a Reaganism."

"Why not. He had a whole stable of screenwriters to borrow from. But let's not stray from the subject. Enlighten me."

"It's routine as far as I'm concerned. We had those reports of UFO sightings and abductions in Arizona. So I had a team sent out there. What's the problem?"

"The problem? The problem is those two idiots you sent out there. They were caught trespassing, posed as government agents without credentials to back them up. Then they made threats as they were being sent packing. Someone out there must have some pull with the President or someone close to him. Anyway, they called collect and complained, wanting to know what's up.

"So, what's up? Have you heard from those incompetent morons?"

"They report to Drew, so I'll call him. But most likely there won't be any report until they complete their mission."

"Well, our beloved Director wants answers ASAP. Which means the Oval Office gave him the same priority. Get on it, Stewart. ASAP."

Stewart put down the phone gently although he wished he could slam it down. Then he picked it up again and punched buttons.

"Drew!" he barked when it was answered. He relished handing down to his subordinates what he had received from his superiors. "What have those two idiots you sent to Arizona done to merit the attention of the White

House?"

"The White House is involved? Look, Stewart. I don't know what, if anything, they've done out there. They haven't reported in and I wasn't expecting them to do so until they finished. What's the flap out there?"

Stewart explained the compliant coming down the chain of command. "The Assistant Director wants an answer, so does the Director in order to answer to the White House, McNamara, I assume. And if I know Mac, the President also knows about it."

"We just sent out a team for a routine check--well, not exactly routine. Our friends down in the basement came across some inquiries about missing persons from Ohio and Kansas, which coincidentally or not, also have the names of some people suspected of having been abducted two to five years ago. The inquiry came from a Jeff Randall, who happens to be an aide to Congressman Truman Sawyer. His district includes the area where Randall is stationed."

"And that's where you sent the team?"

"Yeah."

"What were their orders?"

"Well, you know. The usual."

"You mean--all the way?"

"Look, Stewart, I know these lines are supposed to be secure, but I don't like to discuss these things over the phone.

"How did this get to the White House?"

"Somebody out there has a direct line to the Oval Office looks like."

"Maybe it's this Randall fellow, through his congressman."

"Not likely. Sawyer is a nobody. Even the President doesn't know who he is and they belong to the same party.

"But we're straying again. Start giving me some answers I can pass on."

"I just told you all I know. They haven't come back with any answers."

"Then abort the mission and call them back. If you can't get hold of them, send another team. But in any case, either the mission is completed within 48 hours or pull out all your men. Comprende?"

"Yeah, but I don't know if that is enough time. That area is a quagmire of mountains, valleys, rivers and a forest of dead trees and vegetation. They could be anywhere. And the same for their targets."

"Drew, these requests have all come down ASAP. So 48 hours is pretty liberal on my part.

"'Nuff said. Good-bye, Drew." He put down the telephone and leaned back in his chair. No one below him except Drew knew this was his project and he had only a vague order from the Assistant Director to back him up.

Stewart was not his real name, any more than Drew's was or any of the other men working in the Analyst and Investigative arms of the group. It had been easy in the beginning. Easy to use ridicule to discourage others from going public. And the few who didn't were easy to dispose of. But with time and more people discovering what was going on above their heads, it became harder to ridicule and more care given to disposal methods. There were just so many accidents you could arrange before coincidences would be noticed.

He wondered who had the influence out there to reach the Oval Office.

Then he picked up the phone again.

"Drew," when he got an answer. "Add my name to the list of that team. We have no time to waste. Let's take off this afternoon. We'll fly to Phoenix and I want a chopper made available to fly us to Stonecliff. When we get there, I'll call any reports to you and you pass them to the Assistant Director."

"I don't think this is a good idea, Stewart. If you want my input on..."

"I just said all there was to be said. Have the men meet me in the lobby in one hour. Goodbye, Drew. I'll call you."

CHAPTER TWENTY FOUR

"His full name is James Fenzer, an archaeologist. His wife's name is Dorothy, formerly Perkins, and later Walters. Her old man owned the local supermarket and next to it, a specialty store catering to Western style living, including firearms. The disaster wiped out the town and her father's business. As the only child she got what was left, but the government compensated her for her loss. So neither one is hard up for cash, even though he's not holding down a job right now.

"She's out there on the property every day supervising the rebuilding of the two stores. Her husband helps out, but she's the business brain of the family. They have a home nearby, also courtesy of the U.S. of A.

"The two are part of the group that survived the disaster, forty three in all. They're like a close-knit family and, apparently, all very friendly with each other. Fenzer is the unofficial mayor of the town. Unofficial, because he has never been elected to the post. But from what I learned, he has always been the leader going back to his high school days.

"She's five foot six, about one twenty, green eyes, dark hair, a former cheerleader in high school--in other words a knockout.

"You saw him, so you know he's no wimp. He played football in high school and college. His work has taken him to Mexico, South America and the Middle East. During the late disaster, he held the group together. A group of survivalists tried to take over, but he wiped them out, getting wounded in the process.

"That about sums it up," Mitch concluded, laying down the sheet of paper he had read.

"In other words, not a guy you want to mess with," Jensen whistled.

"We've dealt with worse."

Jensen picked up the paper to look at it. They were having breakfast at a diner. The crowd was thinning, it was almost nine o'clock.

"This thing is kinda short on detail," said Jensen. "I'd like to know more about this fracas he had with the survivalists. How many were there? Did he do it by himself?"

"It doesn't matter. We can do it by ourselves."

"Oh? According to this he has lots of friends, all of whom stick together. Toting arms comes natural around these parts. And if you mess with their women, you might as well stake yourself over an anthill to take the easy way out."

"Jesus, Jensen, I can't believe you. One minute you're panting to take on a bunch that has your back targeted. Next you're looking for excuses to back out because we might encounter trouble from some would-be Rambo."

"I like being careful. I would have been willing to charge up those porch steps against two unarmed men. Anyone out in the dark or inside the cabin would have been reluctant to shoot, fearing to hit their own people. But, here we're planning a caper without any idea of what they're doing or where they are. We could be under surveillance for all we know. They got a good look at our faces at that cabin."

"I doubt it. I've kept my eyes open. I haven't seen anyone overly interested in us."

"Yeah? I saw that guy at the gas station looking over the car."

"Yeah, I remember he said you don't see many cars like ours around here."

"That's the kinda things people remember if they're questioned later."

Mitch laid down his napkin and got up. "C'mon. Quit worrying. Right now is time to start our caper, as you call it."

The parking lot of the Perkins Supermarket was almost full. Part of it held construction materials, trailers and the vehicles of the workers. Closer to the store, spaces had been reserved for the paying customers.

Jensen pull the big car into an empty space near one of the entrances. "Now what? We don't know what she looks like."

"We'll ask."

"Damn it, Mitch. Someone's bound to remember that when she turns up missing. Which brings up another question. What do we do after we grab her and dispose of her. Go back to Washington? They'll be looking for every stranger in these parts, especially her husband and friends."

"Yeah, back to Washington. No way around it."

"Which is what I suggested earlier and you vetoed. What you are doing now is just plain revenge for that humiliation at the cabin. Face it, we underestimated them. We didn't do our research. We thought we were dealing with a bunch of hicks.

"And we still haven't found what we came out here for. We'll have to tell the Great One we failed."

Mitch brushed him off, angrily. "I'm committed to this. Are you with me?"

"We're partners, Mitch. Still, it don't mean I like it."

They got out of the car. Seeing a young man wearing a cap and vest with the store's logo and pushing a cart towards the store, Mitch accosted him.

"Hi! We represent an industry magazine. Our editors

sent us to do an article on the resurrection of the Perkins Supermarket. Could you point out Mrs. Fenzer for us? We've never met her."

"Oh, great. Sure, come on. I'll show you." They went in and the boy looked towards an enclosed area that served as the office. "See those two ladies talking in front of the office?

The one on the right is Mrs. Fenzer."

Both of them were good looking, but the one on the right, Mrs. Fenzer, was definitely the beauty of the two.

A look-alike for Jaclyn Smith, thought Jensen, thinking of his own personal favorite.

"How do we separate her from all these people?" he asked. "Everyone is bound to remember us. We've talked to too many people."

"It won't matter. By this time tomorrow we'll be on the highway headed east."

The two women made the decision for them, heading for the entrance where the two men waited.

"Ah, Mrs. Fenzer?" Mitch saw her up close and was taken by her green eyes. "Could we have a word with you?"

"Do I know you?" she asked.

"No, of course not. We represent an industry magazine. Our readers would be excited to hear how you're bringing your father's store back to life, so to speak."

The four people continued out the door, the two men following because the women had not stopped to accommodate them.

"I'm sorry, gentlemen, but my time is already taken this morning. Come by at one this afternoon and I'll be glad to talk to you."

"I'm afraid that won't be possible, Mrs. Fenzer," Mitch's voice changed. "You're coming with us--and so will the young lady, unfortunately for her."

Each man took hold of a woman's arm and steered her towards the car. "Get in back," Mitch commanded.

When Dorothy hesitated, he tightened his hold on her arm. "Do it!"

She went in, followed by Laura Criden, who was the

other woman.

"What is the meaning of this?" Laura demanded. "Are you kidnapping us?"

Dorothy was quiet, looking at the two men. "I believe, Dr. Criden, these are the two men who were caught sneaking around the cabin."

"What could they possibly gain by taking us?" Laura exclaimed.

"Money is usually at the root of all kidnappings," said Dorothy. "But if they did their proper research, they should know there is none in this town. So it has to do with their attempted incursion at the cabin. Right, gentlemen?"

"You're not in a position to ask questions," Mitch replied.

"Which is a roundabout way of confirming the truth of my statement," Dorothy glanced at Laura.

Jensen started the engine and drove out of the parking lot. Mitch was half turned in the front seat, looking at his captives. "Think what you will, Mrs. Fenzer. It won't matter to either of us."

Dorothy shook her head, turned to Laura. "Why is it that I always end up with these sorry, two-bit excuses for would-be bad guys."

Mitch flushed. Jensen winced.

"Two years ago their names were Larry and Curt," she put her hand over her breast and lowered her head, "now deceased. May God have mercy on their souls."

Mitch smiled. "Very nice. Pity I don't critic acting performances."

"That was no acting. It was a statement of fact. It never ceases to amaze me how people commit dastardly acts while ignoring the eventual consequences. One has to wonder where they carry their brain matter. Certainly not in their heads.

"And speaking of performances, you two certainly deserve a turkey award for that night at the cabin. I wish I could have caught your looks of surprise and consternation on film. Another friend and I were in that cabin with Winchester repeating rifles. So I have to give you credit for retreating gracefully."

Mitch's mouth was now a straight line. Jensen, in spite of himself, had to smile. The woman had guts. "Where are we heading?" he asked Mitch.

"Let's get on that road to the cabin. We're going to find out, once and for all, what they're hiding out there."

"That's a dead end, Mitch. We're wasting time. I don't know how long we have before they notice she's missing."

"You've got three or four hours before they notice," said Dorothy. "Not enough time to get there and back. And your friend's right, Mitch. There's no other road. In fact, it's more of a private road to the reservation. Only some forty people have used that road."

"You can add two more," said Mitch.

"Yeah," Dorothy retorted, "but those forty got to return."

"Who's out there now?" Mitch snarled.

"It varies. But there's usually at least two people there to guard the bullion."

"Bullion!" Jensen exclaimed.

"Of course. The Lost Dutchman's Mine--or is it Jean Lafitte's treasure. I keep forgetting."

"She's pulling your leg," Mitch snapped.

"I would not!" Dorothy smiled. "I only pull my husband's leg--and a great one it is."

"That's enough. You would do yourself and your friend a great favor if you told the truth."

She turned to Laura. "I wish I had Sylvia's memory for great movie lines. I think there's one about not being able to stand the truth.

"I don't know what you think is out there," she turned to Mitch. "I don't know what you're looking for, but you wouldn't believe me if I told you the truth."

"Try me."

"If you're really from the government, you should know this has nothing to do with national defense, state secrets, atomic weapons or any weapon at all. It has to do..."

The engine sputtered, then regained speed. Jensen looked at the instrument panel. A red light had come on.

"We've got trouble," he said. Then he saw it was the fuel indicator. It was on Empty.

"Shit! We're out of gas!"

Mitch whirled. "How can that be? We filled up yesterday evening."

The engine sputtered again, then died.

Jensen steered toward the side of the road and pressed down on the brake pedal. It was down all the way to the floor.

“We have no brakes!”

CHAPTER TWENTY FIVE

Martin dropped off John at his house that morning and continued on to the cabin where Jeff was waiting. After breakfast with Jean, John drove to Jim's house.

"What's up?" Jim greeted him.

John told him how they had located the intruder's car. Then, how he and Martin had placed an electronic bug on the car to keep track of the vehicle.

"Here, look at this. We got it at Gil Borders' shop. Martin has one. We'll keep track from Stonecliff and from the cave area."

Jim was looking at the tracking device, one point which was blinking. "Is that them?"

John nodded. "I made a cross here at the upper left hand corner which represents their motel. For now we'll figure the top of this device as north and go clockwise to east, south and west. When they left their motel, they went south and then made a left turn to Stonecliff which is east in this device. Right now it's stopped because they're at the diner having breakfast.

"We're going to have to put some lines here to represent streets or locations. I've already put in 87 and Main Street where they stopped to eat."

"Look, they're moving. South--right?"

"Have you got a town map, Jim?"

"Not a current one. We've tried to keep the old streets intact. As we cleared them, we put the old names back. So I would say they're heading south on Berman."

"How do you want to handle this? How much surveillance do we do and at what point do we step in and chase them out of town?"

"Much as I would like to know what they want and what agency they represent, I'd leave them alone unless they present a threat to any of us."

"They've already threatened. But, all right. Which one of us tracks them?"

"I'm supposed to meet Dorothy at the store. What are your plans?"

"Martin left me a list of stuff he wants. I was planning to shop for it. And since you're going to the store, I'll go with you and see if Dorothy has any of this stuff at her place."

"All right. I'll follow you to the store. What are our friends doing now?"

"They were stopped on Berman. No, they're moving north looks like."

"Let's go then."

The two vans headed south towards the supermarket. John kept glancing at the progress of the Buick. It was still headed north, parallel with his course south and about two blocks apart.

As he pulled into the parking lot, he noticed the car had now turned east. John frowned. Mentally he tried to place what road the car was now traveling. It was certainly on the eastern outskirts of the town and there was nothing beyond there...

He slapped the steering wheel, took out his cell

phone and dialed the cabin. After a few rings it was answered.

"Hello," it was Jeff.

"Jeff, its John. Has Martin arrived yet?"

"No. Is he on the way?"

John explained what had happened last night and this morning. By now Jim was at the car window waiting for him.

John rolled down the window so Jim could hear.

"Tell Martin when he gets there to activate his device and keep an eye on the road. Our two visitors may be planning a return trip. Let's keep in touch on how this develops."

He got out. Jim asking. "What was that about?"

"Our two friends seem to be heading in the direction of the cabin. I just told Jeff to be on the lookout for them and have Martin try to track them when he gets there, which should be within the hour."

"Damn! Let me find Dorothy. We may have to make a quick trip out there."

They entered the store and headed for the office area.

"Yes, she was here, talking to a young woman. Last I saw of them, they were headed outside," one of the clerks told them.

Going outside, Jim found Dorothy's car. "She hasn't left. Maybe she's talking to the construction people."

"Look," John pointed. "Isn't that Laura's car?"

"Yes it is. I wonder if she is the young lady the clerk was referring to. Let's go check the construction trailer."

Before they could go any farther, a young man came by pushing several grocery carts towards the entrance.

"Hi, Mr. Fenzer. Did you hear they're going to write about the reopening of the Perkins Supermarket?"

"No, I haven't. When did you hear about it?"

"Just this morning. There were two men from this magazine who were looking for Mrs. Fenzer. I guess they found her, but I wonder where they're interviewing her?"

John looked at Jim, then drew him aside. "You think it was our two visitors? That device showed them in this area. Berman Street is the western boundary of this business complex."

"Oh God! If they've got Dorothy..."

"Let's check with the construction foreman to make sure. They could be there."

But a check with the foreman came to naught. The foreman had not seen her since the day before.

"The only other possibility is that they went somewhere to conduct an interview--if they were legitimate journalists."

They went back and found the young man. He confirm that one man was shorter than the other and they were wearing business suits. When asked about a car, he wasn't sure, buthe did have an impression of having seen a large, dark-colored car parked close to the store.

"Let's go!" said Jim.

"We'll go in my van," said John. "Let's find out where they are."

"They're still going out towards the cabin," said Jim as he looked at the tracking device. "Why kidnap her and head for the cabin?"

"Kidnap them," said John. "It looks like Laura is with her. Her car was still in the parking lot and she was last seen with Dorothy. I wonder if they took Dorothy to force her to disclose what has happened at the cave."

"There's nothing to disclose. Unless it was that UFO sighting, which is no great shakes nowadays. Although I do remember they were asking questions about sightings and abductions. What information could we supply that a thousand publications haven't already disclosed?"

"Maybe they figured we had something new to add to the stories."

"True, but if I know my wife, she can be ornery enough not to give them the time of day. Then who knows what they might do to her."

"Ah, Jim. There's something I forgot to tell you. I didn't think it important at the time. Martin and I thought it would be a good joke to play on them."

"Oh no," Jim was concerned. "Is it something that

could affect Dorothy or Laura?"

"I don't know. But it will definitely slow them down. You see, when I was underneath their car placing that bug, I also made some small holes on their brake hose and on the line leading to the fuel pump. Anytime now I expect them to come to a full stop."

"Damn, John! With no brakes they could plunge off the road."

"Maybe. They still have the hand brake. And if they're on this side of the mountain, they'll be going uphill. When the car gives out, they can back up against the side of the road."

“That’s a lot of ‘ifs’, John.”

CHAPTER TWENTY SIX

The car rolled to a stop and Jensen put it in "park."

"Well, that was close," Jensen grunted.

"Yeah, right," said Dorothy. "You are out of gas and going uphill. Who needs brakes?"

"That's just great," exclaimed Mitch. "We kidnap two women and now we're stranded in the middle of nowhere in a car with no gas and no brakes. Great planning."

"I put in gas yesterday. You were there. There was no reason to check the brakes. They worked for two thousand miles. I don't get it."

Mitch opened the door and looked back at his captives. "Get out. We can't stay here. Your friends will come looking for you."

"Yes, my friends," she said. "But it's my husband you should worry about. The last one to try what you've just done is buried somewhere under this road. We figured it was too much trouble to dig him up for a Christian burial. We didn't have the equipment to do so and--well, he was no Christian."

"Enough of the tough guy speeches," snarled Mitch.

"How far are we from that cabin?"

"You said it a while ago. We're in the middle of nowhere. It's some fifty miles to the cabin, the other side of that mountain," said Dorothy. "And it's thirty miles back to Stonecliff. Of course, if you turn the car around, you can probably coast half that distance. That will make it easier on your feet for the rest of the way."

"Oh, you're sharp," grinned Jensen. "Who writes all your material?"

"Is there a shortcut?" Mitch eyed the two women.

"Dr. Criden is a newcomer. She wouldn't know," said Dorothy. "But to answer your question, there is no shortcut from here to anywhere. This road connects Stonecliff with that cabin, in the reservation. There's no other town or even a house between these two points or off the road. This road exists only to connect the town and the reservation."

"You are a fountain of information," Mitch smirked.

"What do you want to do, Mitch?" Jensen asked.

"Are there any vehicles at the cabin?" Mitch persisted.

She hesitated. "Probably."

"Give it up, Mitch," Jensen insisted. "Leave them here. Turn the car and coast back as far as we can. We should have at least two or three hours before they came after them. In one hour we should make it close to Stonecliff."

"Yes, give it up, Mitch," Dorothy couldn't help adding. "Your co-conspirator makes good sense. You've already screwed up two operations. Are you going for three?"

He slapped her.

"Aw, Mitch. You shouldn't have done that," Jensen looked pained.

"I'm tired of her yapping."

"You slapped her because she made sense," Laura spoke up. "Some men can't stand a woman telling them what's true. Your macho sense of superiority couldn't take the criticism."

"This woman," Mitch pointed to Dorothy, "was

kidnapped for a reason. Because she is her husband's wife. You were an afterthought, in the wrong place at the wrong time. The kidnapped are not solicited for advice or commentary."

There was a red spot on Dorothy's cheek, but she never put her hand to it. "You asked questions and I answered. I also gave you what I thought was good advice since you are both strangers here and don't know the terrain and the people. But, you're right. I'll keep my mouth shut and let you screw up on your own."

"Mitch, let's at least get off the road," Jensen pleaded.

"Yeah, let's do that," after a long angry look at Dorothy.

He pushed the two women across the road. "You're right. We can't stay here."

"There isn't too much cover," said Jensen. "The brush is about two feet high with few exceptions. We can crouch down, but even so, they're going to know we went in at this point. The car is a dead giveaway."

"All right. Then go ahead and let it coast down the hill, maybe a mile at least. Then come back. Stay on the gravel, don't leave tracks."

Jensen got in the car and with some push power from the others, let the car coast backwards until it disappeared from view.

It was some forty minutes later that he returned, puffing, and stopped in front of the three waiting for him.

"It's around the curve down there, just off the road."

"Good," said Mitch. "When they find the car empty, they'll have to take time to search the brush area around it."

"And where will we be?" asked Jensen.

"We'll have to go deeper into the brush."

"That's a given," said Jensen. "But where are we headed?"

"I figure if we head north or northeast, we should hit I-40."

"I don't know. Seems pretty far if you're going to walk it. And if the terrain is anything like this, you can double the travel time and the wear and tear."

Mitch looked at Dorothy, but she just stared over his head. "How far is I-40 from here?"

She focused on him now. "You asking me for information? You want advice or commentary?"

"Forget it," Mitch was too proud to back down.

"The women won't have an easy time keeping up with us, Mitch."

"Gee, that's too bad. Maybe we'll have to leave them behind."

"That's what I said all along."

"Yes, but we won't make it easy for them. We'll wait until we've put a few miles away from this road."

They marched into the brush. And it was difficult terrain. The former forest was now all bushland. Here and there, after two years a new one was sprouting up, pushing through the brush and rubble. This was natural reforestation letting nature take its course. But that time was still a decade or two away.

"At least this time my attire is more appropriate," Dorothy told Laura. "Last time we were fugitives from a class reunion. We were wearing our best, cocktail dresses, hose and high heels, to impress our classmates. Before it ended, we got soaked, muddied and our fancy clothes reduced to rags and it took several weeks before we got any replacements." She was wearing jeans, blouse and her shoes had no heels. Laura was more formal with a slack suit and one and a half inch heels. Still, it was manageable, if not the perfect outfit for tramping through the brush.

Mitch kept them moving. At first Dorothy didn't keep track of direction or surroundings. But then, she recognized a landmark. An all too familiar one of two years ago. Then it all came back. Her flight from Larry only to fall into the clutches of Curt. She began to lag back, her hand holding on to Laura, ostensibly for support. In reality, she was slowing the other woman from going too fast.

"What's the matter with you two," Mitch fumed. "Keep up. We have a long way to go."

"Hey! Excuse us weak females for getting tired," Dorothy glowered. "This wasn't our choice for a family outing."

Mitch enjoyed their discomfort. "What happened to the warrior princess act?"

"Warrior princesses get old and used to the good life with the warrior prince."

"Maybe this is a good place to dump our excess baggage," nodded Mitch, looking up. "It's about the noon hour."

"Yeah, and you didn't bring a picnic basket," Dorothy added.

"I don't like this, Mitch. You say that we will hit I-40 if we keep going north, but we don't know what's between here and there and how long it will take. And we have no food or water."

"All right. Suppose you tell me how to get out of this?"

"I don't know if I can. With the car conked out in the middle of nowhere, we've only got our feet to get us out. If the lady is right, we're fifty miles from that cabin where they probably have a vehicle. But it would take two to three days to make it keeping to the brush. And we chance running into her friends coming from that direction.

"If we try returning to Stonecliff, we chance running into those coming from that direction. But we should hear them coming and hide in the brush. We should make Stonecliff by tonight, tomorrow morning at the latest. Then we can see about renting a car and be out of here sometime tomorrow. I think this is our best bet. Especially since we don't know how far it is to I-40 from here. It's got to be as far as that cabin I figure."

"How about the women?"

"The only thing you can do--leave them here. They would slow us down. You could use them as hostages, but I never saw a hostage situation that came up roses for the guys holding them."

"What's to keep them from following us or flagging their friends on the road and telling them our plans?"

"Tie them up. By the time they get discovered, we should be out of Stonecliff."

"There's a better way to assure their silence," Mitch's tone was ominous."

"No, Mitch. We've left too many witnesses back on our trail. They'll know it was us as sooner or later. Let's not add murder. If we tie them up, hide them, we should have clear sailing for at least a day, maybe more. Yeah, and they could also die, tied up. Wild animals could do the trick. Or the weather or starvation if they're not discovered soon enough.

"All right, Jensen. For once we'll do it your way. But what do we have to tie them up?"

"They've got belts. Maybe..." he turned to the two women. "Are you wearing pantyhose?"

"Nope," said Dorothy, raising her pant leg to show bare skin.

Laura colored and Jensen saw her discomfort.

"Take them off, Miss."

When she still hesitated, Mitch spoke up. "We can do the taking if that's what you prefer."

"Look," said Dorothy. "I saw what looks like a hole on that cliff. Why not let her go in there and do it."

The hole on the cliff was off to the side, perhaps a hundred yards away. It was barely visible from where they stood. But Dorothy had been looking for it. She knew it was there because two years ago she had been there, a captive of the survivalists. The irony didn't escape her. She was a captive once again.

"You've got sharp eyes to have spotted that," said Mitch. "Are you sure you're not familiar with this area?"

"I'm not familiar with the details," she lied. "But I'm familiar with the general area. Most of these cliffs and mountains have openings somewhere on their surfaces. Some of the larger openings became shelters for entire Indian towns. They are all over Arizona and New Mexico and are tourist attractions. And I've learned a few things from my husband who is an archaeologist and familiar with geology."

"All right," said Mitch, who still eyed her with suspicions. But what she had said jibed with his knowledge of her husband. "We'll give the lady a little privacy. But no tricks. Otherwise that hole can be your private burial vault."

They hurried on to the cliff's side which Dorothy had now recognized as the survivalist's cave. It was an open cave. Actually a small edition of those that the ancient Indians had built their cliff dwellings.

"Get in there," Mitch ordered Laura.

"I'll go with her," said Dorothy.

"But you stay outside where we can see you," insisted Mitch.

The two women had to climb a gentle slope since the cave opening was not on ground level.

"Could there be any animals in there?" Laura was afraid.

"Probably not. Not too many survived the disaster. Few have returned. Only the insect and fowl species have survived in numbers. But you won't be going in too far."

"I feel like I'm handing them a gun so they can shoot me," Laura groaned.

"It's only pantyhose. Unless you want to call it .45 caliber denier," she laughed, which Laura didn't appreciate.

"Yes, but they'll use it to tie us. We'll be helpless. You seem to be taking this calmly."

"At this point there's not much we can do. But I have confidence in Jim and John finding us."

"Yes, but when?" Laura was now inside, removing her shoes and slacks while Dorothy stood at the opening, her back to the men.

"This cave played a role in my life two years ago. This was the survivalist's camp."

"Oh?"

"I know more about this area then I've let on. I'll tell you more after we find out what their plans are."

"I can tell you that. Tie us up and leave us to starve or be eaten by some wild animal."

"Laura, where is your sense of adventure?"

"Surely you jest. My definition of adventure does not include being tied down and with a snarling bear inches from my face."

She came out waving her pantyhose so that the men at the bottom of the slope could see it.

"I must be dreaming," she said. "This whole thing is unreal. Pinch me and wake me up."

Dorothy patted her on the back. "Atta girl! Go down and don't let them think you're scared."

Laura looked at her. "Now I know why they picked you as cheerleader."

They came down the slope and Laura tossed the pantyhose to Mitch. "It has a run and it's your fault."

"Slip it over your face," Dorothy grinned. "We've got to protect the guilty."

Mitch smiled. "Have your fun, lady. I'll have the last laugh. Tie them up, Jensen. Get them back to back and tie their hands behind them. Use their belts for their ankles."

Jensen nodded. He wasn't too happy. He was quite taken by Dorothy. "Where shall we leave them?"

"Oh, put them in the cave. We wouldn't want them getting wet if it rains. They could catch their death," he turned away laughing.

Jensen took them to the cave and guided them inside.

"Turn around, back to back."

"Look, Dorothy smiled at him. "If we're going to be ties up for a while, let us have a little comfort. I notice there's a patch of ground here where the dirt looks soft. Do you mind putting us there?"

"Sure," Jensen was sympathetic. "Sorry about this. Kidnapping was never my idea."

"All right, I'll forgive you if that's what you want. But we're bewildered. What is this all about? Why are you interested in that cabin? And why kidnap us?"

"It's better you don't know."

"Why not. You're leaving us trussed up like pigs ready for roasting. I'd like to know there is a legitimate reason why I'm giving up my life."

"Don't worry, you'll be found."

"Did we build that cabin over a uranium lode or gold vein?"

"Naw, it has nothing to do with that cabin. It's those

UFOs. They're for real. They're here. We've been warned. They're up to no good."

"That's ridiculous. And you're government, you say? The official position is that UFOs don't exist. That they're..."

"Yeah, yeah. You said it, 'official.' Most of what the government tells you is BS. It's part of the culture. Lies instead of truth. Official government is not for the people. C-Y-A. Cover Your Ass, that's the motto.

"Look, that's enough. It doesn't matter. We have to leave," he touched her shoulder. "They'll come for you." He left. The women heard him sliding down the slope.

And then it became quiet.

CHAPTER TWENTY SEVEN

"Look! They've stopped." Jim was monitoring the progress of the Buick.

John nodded. "The gas. Maybe they ran out of gas. Now we can catch them."

"Maybe. And maybe it's time we call for reinforcements," he pulled out his cell phone. "Jeff. Has Martin arrived?"

"Yes, he's here. We haven't registered the vehicle on this surveillance device yet."

"That's probably because he's stopped on the other side of the mountain.

"Look. We've confirmed the two men have kidnapped Laura and Dorothy from the supermarket. They were headed your way, but now they show as being stopped."

"Laura is with them?"

"Yes, she was with Dorothy. I don't think they

wanted to leave a witness behind."

"I'm on the way," Jeff shouted.

"Bring Martin. I don't think we have to worry about the cabin now."

"We're coming!"

"Well, we have them covered at the pass." Jim put up his phone. "How are the black hats doing?"

"They're still stopped. By now they must know they're out of gas."

"We're coming at them from two directions. If they're out of gas, there's no way to go. They've got to know Dorothy will be missed and her car still in the parking lot. But they may be figuring they have a few hours head start."

"They don't know we have them under surveillance, so we have that advantage. We're about an hour or more behind them. Sooner than they expected us

"Wait! They're coming back!" Jim exclaimed. "What goes on here?"

"Did they drop off the women?"

"It doesn't make sense. Did they make any other stops since they left the supermarket?"

"No. I don't think so. I haven't had my eye on that device full time, but if they made a previous stop, it had to be a quick one. So, no. I'd say they haven't stopped before."

"Then if they're coming back, we should meet them in an hour, less, since they're headed our way."

Three minutes later, John answered him. "Not any more.

They've stopped again."

"Damn! What's going on? I guess it wasn't a fuel problem."

"I'm stepping on the gas. With luck, we should have our answers soon."

There wasn't much conversation after that. Both men kept glancing at the device, but the car didn't change position. After an hour and no change, Jim slapped his knee.

"We should soon know."

"Yeah, but I've got a feeling when we come across that car, it's going to be empty," said John. "It has stayed in that position too long. It has to be out of gas. And that means they would be stupid to stay there and wait for us to show up."

"You're right. And the only way to go is on the road or into the brush."

"With Jeff coming from the cabin and us from Stonecliff, it will be no problem to meet them on the road. Which I doubt they will do."

Jim nodded. "It's into the brush they go."

"With us trailing behind."

Ten minutes later they saw the car. "There it is," John pulled on the side of the road, opposite from where the car was resting.

"It's empty," said Jim as they got out. He went around to the driver's side, opened the door and searched for the lever that would open the trunk. He pulled it.

"Trunk's empty," said John.

"That's a relief," Jim looked in the back. "I can confirm Dorothy was here. I smell her perfume."

"Now we know for sure they were kidnapped and by whom."

"Yeah," Jim was looking at the car. "Something is wrong here. We saw the car stop. Then it came back. The front end points up the mountain, but it is on the wrong side of the road. It's on the right side if you were driving back, but the wrong side if you're driving up the mountain."

John looked and whistled. "Yeah--And notice, it's the rear end that's been run off the road while the front end is still partially on the road. Usually it's the other way around, isn't it?"

"Yeah," Jim nodded. "The front wheels are angled so that the front end would move towards the side of the road. He didn't quite make it."

"That's it!" Jim smacked his fist into his palm. "They stopped the first time because they ran out of gas. Then they had to go into the brush to hide or get away. But the car would be a dead giveaway where they had entered the brush, so..."

"...so, they coasted downhill, driving backward and

dumped it here," John finished for him. "Probably one man did that. That would make us waste time trying to pick a trail from here instead of where the car first stopped."

"They thought they were being smart," John continued. He stepped out on the road and search the ground. "But we outsmarted them with our bug. And now here is the proof," he pointed to the ground, dipping his finger on the road.

"Brake fluid," putting his finger to his nose.

He looked at Jim. "Gas evaporates, but brake fluid hangs around leaving stains. All we have to do is follow the trail. Where it ends is where they made the first stop and most likely where they took to the brush."

"Let's go," said Jim. "I'll drive, you hang out that window and follow the trail. He drove in the middle of the road to allow John a better look at the stains on the road.

"Stop!" John cried. "It just gave out."

They got out and walked back. "Here it is," said John. "The puddle is much larger. This is where they stopped the first time--out of gas and no brakes. It's easy to spot if you're looking for it. Something they didn't figure on."

"Good," Jim crossed the road. "I'll check this side, you check the other. See where they went into the brush.

After a few minutes, Jim hollered. "Here it is. They didn't make an attempt to hide their entry."

"Then let's go after them."

"Wait. They're armed. I'm not. Are you?"

"You know me, Jim. Never go anywhere without my Winchester. It's in the van."

"Great. But first let me make a couple of phone calls. Using the cell phone, he got Jeff. "Where are you?"

"A few miles from the crest."

"Good. We're just over the other side. We've found where they went into the brush when they ran out of gas. I'll tell you that story later. How soon do you figure to make it?"

"Oh, fifteen, twenty minutes."

"Then we'll wait for you. Are you armed?"

"Yep--and aching to use it. Poor Laura, what she must be going through--and Dorothy too."

"Yeah, I know. But Dorothy is no slouch or newcomer to this. She's gone through worse. It doesn't make it easier, but she's dealt with this situation before."

He hung up and punch numbers again. "Mr. McNamara, please. James Fenzer calling from Arizona. He told me to get back to him with some information."

There followed a five minute wait before Jim had a reply. "McNamara here. Is that you? Mr. Fenzer?"

"Yes, I'm sorry to bother you, sir. This is a follow-up to that call I made yesterday. I have more disturbing information for you. Since I made that call, my wife and another woman, Dr. Laura Criden, of the Public Health Services have been kidnapped. We found the car used in the crime. The license plate says 'U.S. Government,'" Jim gave the license number. "The car was abandoned on a private road leading to the Indian reservation. Four of us are starting the pursuit, immediately. You have my number and I have yours. You can reach me any time.

"But, sir, a crime has been committed now. Possibly the lives of two women may be at stake. And the perpetrators are either government agents or posing as such. I think this fits with your concern you had earlier when you first asked me to keep in touch two years ago." He gave a description of the car and the two men.

"Mr. Fenzer, I assure you it is still a concern to me and the President. We don't want a repeat of what happened out there two years ago. No one, especially the President, wants unexpected surprises. I will get someone on this immediately. If someone in this branch of government is involved, I shall be collecting heads.

"I'll be in touch. And you feel free to do the same."

Jim put the phone away. "If McNamara can follow-up on this, then we're closing on these two men from another angle. If they get away from us, maybe we'll get them on their home ground in Washington."

"I'd better make one more phone call and make this official."

He punched numbers again. "Howard? Jim Fenzer. As chief of police of Stonecliff, I'm informing you that my wife and Dr. Criden have been kidnapped. We followed the car, driven by two men who claim to be government agents. We found the car abandoned on the road to the reservation. They've taken to the brush with their captives. Four of us here will be in pursuit within the half hour. Cover your end from Stonecliff. Alert everyone north of here all the way to I-40."

"Will do, Jim. Sorry about Dorothy and the doctor. We'll fence them in. I'll call Phoenix and notify the FBI."

"The FBI may hear about it before you call. But do it anyway. You know my number. Let's keep in touch, Howard."

Howard Manabell, now chief of police, was another of the group of survivors.

The roar of an engine and tires sliding on the gravel signaled the arrival of Jeff and Martin.

"Are we ready to go?" Jeff piled out with Martin close behind. Both were armed with rifles and revolvers.

"Yes, except for one thing," replied Jim. "We're plunging into the brush and leaving two vehicles unguarded.

They could double back, hot wire them and get away. So maybe we should leave one man on guard."

"No problem. We'll remove the distributor caps."

"Yeah, but can you put them back together later?" said John.

“Well worry about that later. Let’s go.”

CHAPTER TWENTY EIGHT

"Mr. McNamara? Childress, FBI. I understand you want to talk to me again?"

"That's right, Mr. Director. Earlier you reported to me in regards to my inquiry of yesterday."

"Yes, sir. And again, let me assure you and the President that we have no operation going in the Stonecliff vicinity."

"Yes. I now have additional information on the subject. It seems that these two men have now kidnapped two women. One is the wife of the mayor of Stonecliff, the other a doctor with The Public Health Service. They used a vehicle bearing government license plates. That number has been given to the Secret Service to find the agency to which it is assigned. Check with them and see where those number point to since kidnapping falls under your jurisdiction. It might help with your investigation.

"And Childress--a little background you should be

aware. And which may explain the President's ire with the intelligence community. Two years ago, during that disaster in Arizona, the previous director of your agency and that of the CIA were prepared to go a little further in their search and disposition of any survivors than what the President ordered.

"That's why you are the Director and your predecessor is gone. That situation in Arizona is not to be repeated, Mr. Director. Whoever those men belong to, if they are government, is on the way to permanent assignment on a deserted Arctic ice floe. Need I say more to describe the President's feelings on the subject?"

"No, sir. I'll have a team sent out from Phoenix immediately. I'll coordinate with the Secret Service on that license number. If we get to them first, we'll have their heads delivered to the White House."

"Good! I like the sound of that. After I hang up, I'll be calling the CIA and giving them the same warning. So you have a three minute head start."

The Assistant Director, his face red, hands shaking, punched numbers on the phone. "Drew! Is everybody bailing out of a sinking ship? Where's Stewart?"

"I don't know, sir. He hasn't called. I presume by this time he should be in a chopper over Stonecliff."

"The White House called the Director and gave him hell for not answering the inquiry. They told him they have the license numbers of a government car that was involved in a crime. It is being tracked by the Secret Service. The agency operating that vehicle will be up shit creek.

"The Director blistered my hide. He swears if it's our agency that's to blame, he will clean house before he leaves. That means, among others, you, me and Stewart."

"Yes, sir. That creek is going to be full of floating bodies. And I can't swim."

"Drew, I'm interested in only one body. Since you can't add anything and Stewart isn't here, who gave you authority to send those men to Arizona?"

"Why, Stewart did. Our investigative group doesn't move until the analyst tell us to."

"And where did Stewart get his authority? He is supposed to go through me. I give final authorization."

"He told me you did."

"What? I don't recall any order for him to send troops to Arizona."

"I can't quote date, time or location because he never told me that. He did make constant references to the AD saying this or that, in reference to the UFO, alien situation. Maybe he thought your conversation constituted your wishes and were an implied, off-the-record authorization."

"I don't do business that way."

"Sir that may be. But you also know that sometimes we conduct some of our business in that manner. It doesn't leave a paper trail that could come back and haunt us like Iran-Contra or Irag-gate. Deny, deny, deny and they can't prove otherwise without it being on the record."

"Yes, yes, all that is true. In our business we have to be careful, otherwise some sanctimonious bastard will pop out of the woodwork and accuse us of being responsible for everything dating back to the Flood.

"But, Drew. Those men are ours. I have to tell the Director and through him, the President. All I can say is that these men turned 'rogue.' That they have not contacted us and that we sent a team to corral them. Let's face it, we have to eliminate them.

"What will be hard to explain is why we sent them out in the first place."

"I think we can safely cover that. We sent them to investigate the UFO, alien abduction reports. What happened after that, we don't know. Maybe their minds were taken over by the aliens."

"Ridiculous!"

"Why not? The tabloids will gobble that up. We need everything to hold up our story. And since more of the public is beginning to believe in flying saucers, that story won't be too hard to swallow."

"What is the true reason, Drew?"

"I don't know. I thought only you and Stewart knew. The men were supposed to go there and discourage and or suppress anyone taking serious this UFO business."

"Even to taking extreme measures?"

"That's usually been the way we work."

"And you didn't question this?"

"Sir, you know the business we're in. We're not always told the reason why we do some things."

"But--UFOs? Isn't it our official position that no such things exist? And if unofficially they do, why don't I know about it? Or the Director? Who does?"

"Maybe Stewart knows. Maybe he's getting his orders from someone not in-house."

"Who? Only the President would have higher authority. But he's the one asking for answers."

The AD's line was silent for a few seconds after his last remark. "All right, we'll go along with that story. We have no choice. Just hope to God it holds up. Otherwise you better put your shredder to work and I'll consult my atlas for a lonely south sea island."

CHAPTER TWENTY NINE

"Nylon stretches. Try pulling away. Maybe we can get some slack," said Laura, following her own advice.

"I think he already took out the slack, Laura.

"But, you feel that soft earth underneath us? Well, that could be our salvation."

"Yeah, right. When it comes time to put us under, they won't have far to go to dig a hole."

Dorothy shook her head. "You don't understand. Two years ago, I was captured by these survivalists. This was their fort. They had the place well-stocked with supplies and equipment for a large group of people. I don't know how many, but there were only eight here, when I was brought in.

"I'll make the story short. Jim and John arrived in the nick of time and rescued me. We got away from them, but they followed and there was a fire fight. That's when Martin blew the mountain. We thought all the bad guys were killed. We came back here and loaded up on the supplies hoarded here.

"We couldn't carry everything, so we buried what we couldn't take, figuring to come back later. Well, other things happened and we never got all we left behind. Some of that stuff is still here, right under us, including firearms and knives."

"No problem," said Laura. "We just dig them up and free ourselves."

"Sarcasm isn't called for, Laura."

"Well, pardon me for wondering how we're going to do that with our hands and feet tied."

"We can't do it with our hands, but we can kick away dirt with our feet. We didn't bury the stuff too deep since we were planning to return soon."

"Well, what the hell, let's try it. It's crazy enough to come true just like everything that has happened lately. Like an unlikely kidnapping, a real, live UFO and an alien abduction."

They commenced kicking away at the soft earth, though their feet were tied together but not to each other as were their hands.

"Everything, especially the weapons were wrapped in a blanket for protection."

"After two years they're probably rusty."

"The firearms were protected by Cosmoline. The knives might be rusty, but they'll still cut.

"Let's try to crawl over there and see if we can sink our fingers in that dirt. Maybe we can feel the blanket."

The President put down the phone and stared at the wall beyond. McNamara watched him but said nothing.

"Nothing. No one knows anything about Arizona," he looked at his chief-of-staff. "Unless..."

"Charles. There's one more source to check. I hope to God it isn't involved.

"Ah, I have to make the call in private. You understand, Charles?"

"Yes, sir. It's been quite a while since you had to

make one of those. Are you sure I can't be cleared to know what's going on?"

"You probably could if I pushed it, but there's too many already and it's not something I want to add to anyone's conscience."

"Very well, sir. I'll be in the outer office if you need me."

When he was alone the President picked up a special line and punched a number.

"Yes, Mr. President?"

"Henry?"

"I should hope so, sir. No one else is supposed to answer this phone."

"It pays to be sure nowadays. Even a president cannot command privacy any more. Ask several of my predecessors.

"And speaking of predecessors, that's why you are where you are and I am stuck with this damnable secrecy."

"Has something come up, sir?"

"I hope not. That's why I'm checking with you. I have some good people, friends of mine, I hope, in Arizona. They have reported harassment by some men purportedly representing the government. They were in search of UFOs and alien abduction rumors. They threatened these people. Now these same men have kidnapped two women, including a government employee.

"I have questioned the usual suspects. CIA admits to sending two men to the area on what they call a routine check of UFO sightings. We have connected a government vehicle in the area as the one used to abduct the two women. The vehicle was assigned to the CIA.

"Now, my question, Henry. Does anyone in your group have some connections with the CIA and using some of their people to do your snooping?"

"Not that I know--wait, yes. Conner used to be in the CIA. In fact, he was assistant director under one of your predecessor's administration. He assigned Conner to the group. Nine of our group are holdovers from previous administrations. Because of the secrecy, this group is continuous in nature, sir. You know that. Only the death of a member removes him from the group. And you and five of your predecessors still alive are the only others who know."

"Is it possible this Conner or any other member of the group have gone out on their own?"

"I don't know that. And I hope it's not true. Everyone here has the highest clearance. But naturally there have been differences among us. The sharpest one being over how long we should continue this secrecy. We may need you to mediate or make a decision one way or another."

"This Conner person--how does he lean?"

"He doesn't lean. He is all for continuing the status quo."

"The secrecy, in other words."

"Yes--he and a few others."

"What is your thinking on this?"

"I agree some things should be public knowledge. Other aspects should remain secret. At least until we know more--and how the public will greet such revelations."

"So much for our side. What about 'them'?"

"Your guess is as good as mine, sir. You've met them.

"They're willing to work with us. But they're very singular in their purpose. They're not politicians with a constituency to satisfy or with personal ambitions to win and remain in public office. It's the perfect society that we preach and proclaim for our democracy, but which we've failed to match the rhetoric with deeds."

The President gave an audible sigh. "Yes, Henry, I'm well aware of that, but we don't live in a society of robots. Some of the men who have occupied this office may have had the highest regards and ideas for what this country should do, but, unfortunately, that's not the way our system has evolved. And I'm not sure I'd want it any other way. Somehow the idea that one man or one group should dictate what the rest should do, still runs against the grain. And didn't we fight a few wars to avoid just that?

"But, we're getting away from the subject. I don't want this secrecy to get out of hand to the point the government, through its agents, has to commit a crime in order to preserve it. And especially not against those people in Arizona. I want to know if anyone in your group is pushing this out of misplaced zeal or personal agenda. Somewhere along the line, a person or persons, has lost control and taken off on their own. If it's originating in your group, Henry, I want it stopped. And I want the name of the culprit. We can't afford to have someone like that working with us."

"If he's one of us, we may not be able to afford to let him go--with all he knows."

"Then he presents that much of a danger, in or out of the group. Then I shall make my decision.

"I'll expect your call, Henry."

"Yes Sir, goodbye Sir."

CHAPTER THIRTY

The four men had been following the trail for quite some time now. Earlier John and Martin had identified the four sets of tracks as two men and two women.

"Of course, who else could it be," said Jim. "No one in this area is dumb enough to plunge into this brush country without a damn good reason."

"But where are they headed?" Jeff wondered. "What's out here?"

"Nothing. That's just it," said John. "Their transportation gave out. Their abduction would soon be discovered, so they had to get away. Trouble is, they don't know this country, so they don't have too much of an idea where they're going."

"They're headed east to northeast," said Martin. "But there's no town this side of the New Mexico border. Not anymore there isn't. Their best bet would be to hit I-40 and get picked up by someone."

"If Howard alerted all peace officers in the state, an alarm may already be in place to look out for them," said

Jim.

"These aren't outdoor types," said John, "and they're hampered by two captives. We should be able to catch them. Especially since they didn't expect us to miss the women so soon."

A short while later, Jim stopped, looking at a towering sandstone cliff ahead. "I know where we are--and possibly where they're headed."

"What is it?" asked Jeff.

"It's the survivalist's stronghold," Jim looked at John. "It's in the cliff ahead."

"Yes, but do they know that?" John replied.

"Dorothy does."

"What are you saying? That Dorothy would lead them there? What would that accomplish?"

"I don't know. That puzzles me. The only thing that would make sense is that Dorothy got them to thinking of it as a hideaway. Then we could follow them here."

"I can't see them buying that. Unless they're utterly stupid."

"These men have been doing stupid since they got here," said Jim. "Makes you wonder if they really belong to some intelligence outfit."

They were at the foot of the cliff and Jim led them to the opening.

"They're up there," said Martin. "Or they were. There's tracks going up and down."

He and John bent down, studying the indentations left by the visitors. Then they looked at the cave which showed no signs of life or movement.

"The tracks of the women show them going up and down," said John. "In fact, it looks like there's two sets of tracks of the women going up and one set coming down. And for the men, one set going up and one set returning."

He looked at Martin. "You agree?"

Martin nodded, then glanced at Jim. "They went up twice. Came down once. Doesn't look good, Jim."

"Then they're up there."

Neither Martin nor John answered.

"Let's get up there," Jim started up the slope.

Martin cocked his rifle. "I'll stay here in case a man's head pops up while you all are climbing."

The three men had no problem climbing the incline towards the opening. All stopped at the top, peering in. It was empty. John put out his arm to keep the others from entering.

"Let me look around first."

He went in, hugging the side of the cave to keep from overlaying his own tracks on those already on the floor of the cave. Only on visibly clear floor, did he step away from the wall. He checked the indentations on the soft part of the cave floor. He also found the pantyhose. Looking at it, he frowned and then beckoned to the others. By now Martin had joined them.

"They were here all right," he held up the pantyhose.

"But there's a conflicting story here.

"Martin, you want to look and back me up?"

Martin nodded and stepped in gingerly as John had. After a few minutes of bending over, running his hands over portions of the floor, he looked to the others. "Tell us what you see, John."

"Apparently one of the women's pantyhose was used to tie them. See, it's all stretched out and you can see several places where it was knotted. But the strange thing is that in spite of that, the hose is complete. That is to say, it hasn't been cut or torn in any way.

"Have you ever taken nylon, put knots in it and then try to undo them" It's almost impossible. But here we have two women tied up, either together or individually and there's some sharp rocks around that could have cut the nylon. Now the women are gone and their nylon bond remains, uncut, but unraveled. If the hose was used to tie them, how could they have undone the knots with their hands tied?"

"They must belong to Laura," said Jim. "I'm almost certain Dorothy wasn't wearing any. She had jeans and flat shoes. She wouldn't wear hose with that outfit. She liked her comfort."

"Look over here," continued John. "On this piece of soft ground. There's a perfect indentation of a pocket on a pair of jeans, even to the button. That means the wearer was lying down. It wouldn't leave that good a print if she were sitting.

"Then you also have these furrows. One or both were pulled or most likely they dragged themselves on the floor.

"See, the furrows are interrupted. They were tied to each other, so they pushed themselves with their legs, then planting their feet, they arched their bodies a couple of feet, then repeated the process. They ended up on that soft concave spot on the floor.

"Ah, Jim, looks like something was buried here. The dirt is too soft and loose."

"Oh, no!" exclaimed Jeff. "They killed them. They're buried here."

"No! No! Wait!" Jim cried. "I know this place. That ground there. Oscar and I dug that hole--two years ago.

"Here," he knelt on the floor and started digging with his fingers. After a few moments, the others joined him.

About two feet down, he felt something soft. "This is it." He ran his fingers over the object until he found an edge. He started pulling. The others exchanged looks, then pitched in to help.

All together they pulled a blanket covered bundle, suspiciously long enough to be a body. But their fingers told them a different story. The object underneath the blanket was too hard. They pulled it out of the hole and Jim unwrapped it. What was revealed were about a dozen rifles and shotguns.

"There's your bodies," said Jim. "Oscar, Dorothy and I were here two years ago. After Martin blew up the mountain, we came here to check for survivors. John went over the mountain to look for Martin--remember?

"Anyway, the three of us returned to Stonecliff, taking what we could carry. What we couldn't, we buried. That's what this is."

"Well, that's a relief," said Jeff. "But where are they?"

"That's the question," said John, "and the puzzle.

They're not here now, but they were. The pantyhose is proof of that. From what Jim said, it had to belong to Laura. But as I observed before, how could a woman, or even two, manage to untie a knot or knots from nylon material? No cuts. No rips. All this while they were tied with said nylon."

"I grasp what you mean, John," said Jeff. "But the alternative is that someone untied them."

"Yes, but by whom? Where are they? We didn't see them on the way here and they didn't see us--and where is this person that untied them? Is he taking them away? And to where?

"Let's suppose Jeff Randall--or any of us--come in here. He sees two women bound, so he sets about freeing them. But it's not easy to untie nylon. My reaction would be to cut it. What would you do? The women are tired, cramped and hungry. Why prolong it by trying to untie them. Do you tell them, 'Fear not, my fair lady, I'll save your pantyhose.' Then he proceeds to take, God knows how long, to untie the damn thing."

The others smiled at John's last line.

"John's right," said Jim. "I can't find fault with his reasoning. But since there's no sign of another person being here, then they untied themselves or the two men took them.

"But," he answered himself, "why would they bring them up here, tie them up, then untie them and take off again?"

"We're wasting time," said John. "Let's look around and see if we find a trail leading away from here."

"What about these weapons? Shall we take them?" Jeff asked.

"We don't have anything to clean off that Cosmolene," said Jim. "And they would load us down. We'll bury them again."

Twenty minutes later, John and Martin found the trail of the two men.

"How about the women?" asked Jeff.

"No sign of them," said John. "All we have from them is two sets of tracks going up that slope, but only one coming down."

"Exactly where we came in," said Jeff, gloomily.

"And where shall we go from here?" John looked at Jim.

"We follow the men. What other choice have we?"

"But the women aren't with them--unless they are carrying them."

"That bothers me a hell of a lot," Jim kicked the dirt.

"When we catch them, they'll supply the answers."

"There's one other possibility," said Martin, looking at the others. “I think you knew which one I mean.”

CHAPTER THIRTY ONE

"Stonecliff ahead!" the chopper pilot announced over the "whupping" sound of the rotor blades. Stewart and the other two men looked out from the craft.

"What do you want me to do?" the pilot asked.

"How much time do we have before refueling?" Stewart asked.

"Couple of hours."

"Good, circle over the town while I make a call."

"Drew!" he exclaimed when he made his connection. "Give me the latest."

"All hell has broken loose. Where are you?"

"Circling over Stonecliff. Give me the bad news."

"The Oval Office is giving the Director hell and he has passed that on to the Assistant Director, than me. They want you. Come back. You have a lot to answer for."

"Can't do that right now, Drew. I have to find those two idiots."

"Then you might be interested to know that those 'two idiots' kidnapped the wife of the mayor of Stonecliff and a doctor with the U.S. Health Services They did all this using a government vehicle which has now been traced to us. The last report we have indicates the vehicle was abandoned on a lonely road which is more or less a private one since it connects only to the Indian reservation some eighty miles east of the town."

"Any reports on where they went after they left the car?"

"Best info is that they fled into the brush with the two women. The police have alerted the whole state. The FBI is on the way--or may already be there. There may not be an agency to come back to, given the attitude at the White House."

"All right, Drew. I'll be in touch."

"Wait! What will I tell them? The Director and the AD. They'll have my ass if they find out you called and I didn't alert them."

"Then don't say anything about it. I won't. Loose lips, you know. Goodbye, Drew."

"Wait! Dammit, Stewart..."

He hung up and turned to the pilot. "Head east. There's supposed to be a single road out that way--a private road. No traffic. Should be easy to find."

After a few minutes. "That must be it. Seems like the only road out of this town going east. But I don't know about the traffic. I see about a dozen cars headed in that direction," said the pilot.

"Let's get past them," said Stewart, "and keep your eyes peeled for two men and two women, probably in the brush area."

The other two men in the chopper had been quiet. Watkins and Gould were their names. They joined in the watch.

"There's three vehicles on the road ahead," said Gould.

"Two vans and a dark four-door sedan."

"Yeah, the sedan I recognize," said Stewart. "Go down low to make sure and see if anyone is in them."

The chopper went down, hovering off to the side of

the cars and whipping up dust and brush. Stewart saw the government license plate on the sedan and the absence of human activity inside the vehicles.

"All right, that's the car, but it's empty. They're somewhere out there. Let's go find them."

"You planning to pick them up when you find them?" the pilot asked. "This thing won't carry four more."

"Look, Steffan. I'll make the decision when we find them. I don't know how many I'll take--if any at all."

"Mr. Stewart, I work for the Agency, but I'm not into the big secrets. If this is an ordinary rescue effort, we can locate them and pass their position to those people in that caravan coming up the road. I suspect that's why all those cars are headed up this road."

"The last thing we want to do is hand them over to who-ever is coming in those cars."

"O.K., I get it. It's none of my business. I'm just the bus driver."

"You've got it, my friend. Now let's find those idiots before the villagers get to them."

Mitch and Jensen were crashing through the brush. "Are we headed in the right direction," Jensen gasped.

"We're headed in the opposite direction that those four men were. How in hell did they get out here so fast? They're about an hour behind us when it should have been half a day.

It's like we left a trail of bread crumbs."

"A trail of brake fluid, for sure."

"Look! There's their cars. Great! That's what I call justice. We'll take theirs."

They plunged out to the road only to pull up short as they saw the upraised hoods.

"What the hell happened?" Mitch snarled.

Jensen looked under the hood. "They took the distributor caps."

"Bastards!" Mitch yelled. "We can't use them--Well, neither can they," he pulled out his gun and aimed for the engine.

But Jensen leaped forward and stopped him. "No! They'll hear the shot. They can't be too far behind us. Let's get going--on the road. We can make better time and leave no trail."

Mitch was still angry, but allowed himself to be led away, the wisdom of Jensen's remarks blowing away the anger.

"All right," he expelled his breath. "Let's go."

They jogged back towards Stonecliff until the curve of the road hid the stranded vehicles. Then they slowed to a fast walk. "I'm not in shape for this," complained Jensen.

"Who is? Except for those health nuts. We've made a real mess of this."

"'We'?" Jensen couldn't help saying.

"All right. Don't give me that, 'I told you so.' I never had a job like this before. These hicks have been sticking with us like fleas on a dog."

Jensen stopped. "You hear that? Cars coming."

"Back to the brush!" Mitch shouted. They scrambled off the road and threw themselves flat on the ground.

A few minutes later a line of vehicles appeared and roared by, spraying gravel in their wake.

"I counted eleven vans and pickups," said Jensen.

"The whole population of Stonecliff, no doubt. Coming to the aid of their buddies.

"C'mon. The way should be clear into town."

"Yeah, but will my feet hold up. It must be at least a three hour walk--if we don't encounter any more traffic."

"It's almost five o'clock," Mitch checked his watch.

"Maybe a couple of hours of daylight left, so long as we stick to the road or close to it."

They plodded on, showing signs of fatigue. It was the legs that were aching, not to mention shortness of breath by Mitch. And no food since breakfast.

Some twenty minutes later they heard a new sound. Whup! Whup! Whup!

"Oh God!" exclaimed Jensen. "They've got a chopper after us."

"Damn! And no place to hide."

Apparently they had already been sighted because the craft was coming in low.

Someone leaned out and addressed them through a loudspeaker.

"Don't move! We're picking you up! Don't resist. We're friends from Washington. Wave your arm to show you understand."

Jensen looked at Mitch. "What do you think?"

"We don't have much choice, do we? Out in the open. We can't outrun them," Mitch raised his arm and waved.

The helicopter slowly settled to the road and a man hopped off.

"Oh, my God!" Mitch exclaimed. "The Great One himself. Have we been saved?"

"I'm not going to argue the point or purpose. My legs can't hold out much longer"

Stewart waved them towards the craft. "Hurry up! Get in! We don't have much time."

He shook hands with each as they boarded. "It's going to be a tight squeeze unless one of you wants to stay behind."

"No thanks," said Mitch, scrambling ahead of Jensen. After a shifting and repositioning of bodies, the chopper took off. Stewart, sitting in front with the pilot, turned around and made the introductions.

"There's a lot we have to talk about," he looked at the newcomers. "You two are in deep shit. But, right now, since we're already on the scene, let's finish what we started. Later on, we'll have a report in private.

"Now what were your instructions? What did you do and what was left undone?"

Mitch explained what had happened from their first appearance at the cabin and their inability to get any further information on sightings or abductions. He left off the kidnapping, although everyone knew about it except for the 'why.'

"Where is this closely-guarded cabin from here?"

"No problem. Just follow the road going east."

Stewart turned to the pilot. "You heard?"

He nodded and banked the craft around to head east. On the way they passed the caravan of vehicles which were now stopped by the three stranded vehicles on the road.

"You know who they are?" Stewart asked the two.

"Not sure, but probably a posse from Stonecliff."

"Yes. That too will require explanation in private."

Thirty minutes later, they hovered over the cliff, at the base where the cabin stood. Mitch had given directions to the pilot who now asked for further instructions.

Stewart turned to Mitch. "Now, what exactly did you find and your conclusions that led to these subsequent, ah, problems?"

"You've got a good-sized, well-equipped cabin in the middle of nowhere. For what? You build a warning system, motion detectors and banks of lights to rival a ball park.

"What is out here? What are they hiding? And they are well armed."

"I don't think you can put too much stock on the firearms," said Watkins. "That's standard procedure out in these parts. It would be suspicious if someone didn't own any."

"Maybe so, but combined with the other oddities, I think it's something to make us suspicious," replied Mitch.

"But how does all that tie in with UFOs, which you were supposed to investigate?" said Stewart. "Did you check with the local natives to see if they knew about this and what the story was--if any?"

"No, we never got to that. We..." Mitch stammered as Jensen watched, offering no help.

"No, of course not," replied Stewart. "You went into your extracurricular mode. Right?"

Mitch was spared an answer as the pilot interrupted. "We're wasting fuel waiting here. I've got just under an hour left to get us back in time to refuel. So give me some instructions."

"Let's land and make a quick inspection of the premises."

"We're trespassing, you know," Jensen put in."

"And?" from Stewart.

"Just to let you know how all this got started and six people are now crowded in this closet, trying to straighten this out."

"All right, Jensen. Your view has been heard and there are five witnesses for the record. Put her down, Steffan."

The chopper started to descend towards the canyon where the cabin was located, the wall of the cliff to their right.

Then the top of the cliff started shimmering like a picture going out of focus.

"What the hell!" the pilot exclaimed. "What's going on? Is it me or is there something wrong on top that cliff?"

The others craned their necks to look and then uttered exclamations, rubbing their eyes.

"It's out of focus--blurred," said Stewart. "Is that what you mean?"

"Just the top of the cliff. The ground below looks all right," replied the pilot.

"I told you there was something strange over here," said Mitch.

"Looks like something you would read in science fiction--a force field of some sort," said the pilot.

"Hey! The chopper seems drawn to it!"

The craft was now tossing violently, veering towards the top of the cliff instead of the ground around the cabin.

"We're going to crash!" one of the men shouted.

The helicopter was now plunging towards the top of the mountain which the pilot couldn't make out because the landscape was blurred and shimmering like heat in a hot summer day.

Then the plunge stopped and the chopper seemed to float down. "I don't have control!" screamed the pilot.

The ground came up. It suddenly cleared. But the ground was completely changed from how it had looked earlier. Right below and being drawn to it, was a giant space ship.

“Oh God,” said Jensen. “We found the Secret!”

CHAPTER THIRTY TWO

The men were clustered around the abandoned vehicles. They had all been called together by Howard Manabell, the police chief.

Long ago, when Stonecliff started to rebuild, it was evident that a large police force was unnecessary, the town being short on population and hardly any crime worthy of the name. So it was decided that in case of emergencies, citizen volunteers would help as auxiliaries. At least a score had responded upon learning of the kidnapping of the popular Dorothy and the respected Dr. Laura.

The two empty vans had already been identified as belonging to John and Martin. Howard had filled in the others with the details.

As they stood there, the helicopter came by and swept over them without stopping. Howard inspected the craft with his binoculars.

"Strange. No markings on it," he observed. "It can't be media. They would have stopped."

"Maybe it was the FBI," said Oscar. "You did call

them, didn't you?"

"Actually, they called me. It seems Jim was in touch with the White House in regards to that government car over there."

"What's the story behind it?" Aaron asked.

"I don't know except that the two men driving it kidnapped Dorothy and Laura."

"They're coming!" someone shouted.

Jim and his companions appeared at the side of the road and were greeted by their friends.

"Did you find them?" Howard asked.

"No. We found where they had been. They're still missing. But we tracked the men back to this point. I don't suppose you've seen them?"

"No," Oscar answered for him. "No one else has come out of the brush in the last thirty minutes. The whole bunch of us drove in from town and we met no one on the road or here."

Jim's shoulders slumped. He looked around his circle of friends, Oscar, Aaron, Howard, Linda, Sylvia, Esther, Carl, David and Nancy, Jean--the latter rushing to John's side.

"She's gone--And I have no idea where to look for her." Oscar came over and put his hand on Jim's shoulder. "Tell us all about it. Maybe we can help."

"They disappeared at the survivalist's cave. It was only the two men we trailed," he slammed his fist against the fender of the nearest car. "Let me be the one to say it. She and Laura may have been killed."

"If that were true, Jim," said John. "We would have found the bodies. But we found nothing. The last place they were, was in that cave."

"Jim," Martin took his arm, "their disappearance is inexplicable, but there is one other explanation, in view of my own experience."

"I can't believe you're serious."

"It's serious enough until you come up with a better explanation.

"Their disappearance cannot be explained. I think

those two men left them tied up in that cave. Then they made their escape. They didn't expect us so soon and if it hadn't been for that tracking device, only now would we be missing them.

"But all the evidence shows they never left that cave again by conventional means. There are no signs of struggle, violence or even blood. That's why I advanced my own explanation."

"I'm sorry, my friend," Jim replied. "I didn't mean to sound off like that. I guess I don't want to think of that angle because it puts me in a helpless situation where I cannot do anything."

"Where do you want to go from here?" Oscar asked.

Jim turned to Howard. "You have someone in town you can contact?"

"Yes, I have my two deputies."

"O.K. Call them and tell them to be on the lookout for the two men. The rest--well, it's up to you guys. I'm going to the cabin. Maybe, like Martin said, I might find some answers there.

"God! I can't lose Dorothy."

"We'll all go," said Aaron, looking at the others for confirmation or negative feedback. There was none.

The distributor caps were replaced on the vans and the caravan set out for the cabin.

"Do you realize there's thirteen cars in this convoy?" Sylvia commented.

"What?" Oscar looked at her. "Are you branching out from the entertainment field into the psychic?"

"Well, it would be a good time, you big oaf. Dorothy is gone. Jim is a wreck and the rest of us are not far behind."

Oscar made no response.

Jim was in the van with Jean and John. "What do you think of Martin's idea?"

"It's as good as any," said John. "He's right, though. We found no evidence of violence, except they were tied up. And then they were let loose. The two men tied them up and left them there. After that, we're left with only two possibilities. They managed to untie themselves or someone else did. The condition of that pantyhose suggests it was someone else. But in either case, what happened after they were untied? Dorothy knew the way back. Why didn't we meet her on the trail? If it was someone else, what did he do with them? There were no signs of a trail where they left or of bodies killed or buried. So, the mystery remains."

"Do you realize that if Martin is right, I might never see her again? What's the history of people abducted? A few hours? A day? Or years like Martin?"

"Better ask Jeff, he's up on those kind of things."

It was six thirty when the procession arrived at the cabin. The canyon was already in shadows as the towering sides of rock on both sides shut off the sunlight.

"We have enough food to feed everyone," said Martin. "In fact, you can stay the night if you want to, otherwise you won't get back until late tonight. The women can stay in the cabin, the men can rough it outside or in the cave."

They looked around at each other as if waiting for someone to utter the first word that would decide for all of them.

"Why not," Aaron shrugged. "But if you've got the sleeping bags, I want my wife with me."

"Sure, got plenty of those," said Jeff. "Martin has everything except for the proverbial kitchen sink--and given enough time, I'm sure we'll be able to pipe in water from the pool."

"While you guys are preparing the food," said Jim, "I'll check inside the cave."

"I'll go with you," said Martin.

Everyone stopped what they were doing to watch them go. But it was only one person that was their greatest concern.

Sylvia and Esther were misty-eyed.

"Jim is all broken up. Theirs's was a love that couldn't be broken. Even in public, those two always eyed and touched each other in a manner that would have drawn an X rating label," said Sylvia.

"Two years ago when Larry kidnapped her and then

when she was taken by the survivalists, we always had a trail to follow her," John ruminated aloud. "But this time there was nothing, no sign where she might be or even if she's alive. This is awful. She was like a sister to me."

Jean hugged him. "I know. She had become our dearest friend."

"Was? Had?" Nancy exclaimed. "Why are you talking about her in the past tense?"

"Like 'Love Story,'" said Sylvia.

"Shut up, Sylvia!" Esther glared at her.

Howard made some more calls to town. There were no reports of anyone sighting the two men. He called other members of the class, telling them what had happened and where they were spending the night. He called the airport and inquired about the use of a helicopter to search the area and was promised one. There was no information on the strange helicopter that had buzzed them. In fact, radar had lost track of the chopper shortly after it had passed over them.

Howard relayed all the information to the others and Jim and Martin when they returned. They had found nothing.

"The airport has reported a possible crash of a chopper close to this location. Probably it's the same one that buzzed us earlier. It went off radar at 5:21 which is shortly after it passed us."

"That's an idea," said Jim. "A helicopter could lift people off the ground. It could explain why Dorothy and Laura left no sign."

Howard shook his head. "That chopper came from the west and going east. If it had picked them up, taken them to Stonecliff, why hasn't anyone in town reported their return? That chopper came from the west going east, southeast which is where it went off the radar. If it was carrying Dorothy and Laura, it could have stopped on the road where we were.

“There's no way they could have missed us and if the women were aboard, they could have told their rescuers to drop them off. So, I doubt that craft had the women."

"It had no markings, you said," Jim observed. "Aren't

all aircraft supposed to have identification?"

"Yes, but if you work for the right people, you can get away with it."

"One of these secret agencies, huh? Where have I heard that before," said Jim.

Howard explained his plan for the following day. "I thought tomorrow morning we make a search of this area, then travel back towards town searching the road and brush.

"I've called the rest of the class for reinforcements. They will be coming in tonight and we'll get an early start."

Jim clapped him on the shoulder. "Thanks, Howard. And thank you, all of you, for your support," he told the others.

"Well, you did a lot for all of us, two years ago and since then," said Oscar. "And it's not payback either. We all have the highest regard and love for Dorothy. She is family. We're all family. When one needs help, all of us pitch in."

"Thanks guys," Jim managed to say, his voice shaking with emotion. Then he strode off in the darkness.

Oscar started after him, but Martin held him back. "I think this is one time a man requires no company. It might be embarrassing if he has to shed tears."

Several more cars arrived later. They had already eaten, but they brought in extra supplies for tomorrow's search.

Jim returned and got the quiet sympathy of the newcomers. It was almost midnight when everyone dropped off to sleep. There were no guards. Everyone was too tired—a long day for everyone.

The First Children had come together.

So it was, there was no one awake to notice that the dark sky gradually lightened and a humming sound grew louder.

CHAPTER THIRTY THREE

She awoke. Saw nothing. She blinked her eyes several times. Still nothing--everything was black. Her hand came up and touched her forehead and then her nose. Eyes wide open, her hand in front of her, she could not even see her hand. She felt her body--fully clothed--felt where she was lying--ground, soft dirt. She pulled herself to a sitting position. Where was she? She was not claustrophobic, but her inability to see made her feel enclosed, imprisoned.

Breathing heavily, she realized she was hyperventilating. She reached out to steady herself and touched human flesh, a body. Then a hand grasped her arm. She screamed.

"Who is it?" a man's voice, groggily.

"What?" a woman's voice.

"It's dark--I can't see!" another woman's voice.

"Oh God! Now I know how the Man in the Iron Mask felt," Sylvia! No one could mistake her voice.

She called out softly. "Sylvia? Is that you?"

There was a moment's silence. "Dorothy?"

Then another voice she could never forget. "Dorothy!"

It was Jim.

Someone started to move and immediately produced a yelp. "Watch it! That's my leg you're stepping on."

"Who's got a light? We need light!"

There was a hubbub of voices.

Dorothy, now reassured she was not alone, called out. "Jim! Where are you?"

"Here! Oh God! Dorothy, it's you!"

Suddenly a light came on as someone struck a match. It was Martin. Everyone could see his face--and the surroundings. It was the cave--and nearby was the pool.

"Everyone stay where you are," Martin ordered. "I'll get lights. I know where they are." Striking matches to light his way, he climbed up the steps to the balcony and disappeared.

"How did we get here?"

"The last I remember, I fell asleep. I was so tired."

"This is weird," you couldn't mistake Sylvia's voice. "Carl, where are you?"

"Right here, next to you."

"Thank heaven, Carl," it was Oscar's voice. "When all I heard was Sylvia's voice, I thought I was in Hell."

The several matches struck by Martin had been enough for Jim to locate Dorothy and he had been trying to move in her direction.

"Dorothy!" it was Jeff. "Where is Laura?"

"Right here! Next to Dorothy," the lady answered for herself. It was her hand that had grasped Dorothy's arm.

Someone else struck a match and that was enough to get Jim and Dorothy together.

"I couldn't find you," Jim gasped as they clasped each other, lips locked in a long and hungry kiss. "I thought I had lost you."

Light now appeared on the cave balcony. It was Martin, carrying a torch. He had a bag of flashlights which he started to distribute to the others.

Jeff came up to Laura, pulled her up and hugged her.

"You're all right?

"Yes," she stared at his eyes, inches away from hers. She saw the concern--then he kissed her.

Taken by surprise, it took several seconds before she reacted. Then she returned the kiss and her arms went around his neck.

The chamber was now lighted well enough that faces could be distinguished and spouses could be united. It also enabled a head count.

"The whole class is here?" Dorothy noted in surprise.

"You and Laura disappeared, so we were all looking for you," Esther replied.

"But, the whole class," Dorothy was touched.

"Yeah," Sylvia had to have her caustic remark. "We were all looking for poor little you."

Oscar laughed. "You made her miss a rerun of 'My Mother, the Car.'"

"Thank you for the extreme sacrifice," Dorothy patted her on the head. "I hope you remembered to tape it."

"I hate to break up the fun and games," said Aaron. "But, look around here and explain how we all got here. The last I remember, Linda and I were in our sleeping bag outside the cabin. I don't recall moving in here."

"You ever sleep walk, Aaron?" Tom asked.

"Well, if I did, so did forty others. Everyone was sleeping in the cabin or outside it."

That sobered everyone.

"Aaron is right," said Oscar. "Why are we all in here? And especially Sylvia who's afraid of snakes in the dark?"

"Also in daytime," added Carl.

No one had an answer.

"Dorothy and Laura are here," said Jim. "Yet Martin and I checked the cave yesterday evening, including this area. They weren't here then."

"Then sometime later, between the time we fell asleep and now, something happened," Jeff put in. "And we were unaware of it."

Jim turned to Dorothy. "We haven't heard your story. You want to tell us about it?"

She told them, beginning with the kidnapping at the supermarket and ending with them tied at the cave.

"I remembered the arms cache and was hoping we could dig up a knife to cut our bonds. But, that's the last I remember. I must have fallen asleep. Next thing I know, I wake up here, pitch black so I couldn't see my hand in front of my face. Something grabbed my arm and I screamed."

"And that was me," said Laura. "I can't add to what Dorothy has told you."

"The common thread seems to be that everyone fell asleep and woke up here," said Jeff.

"It doesn't make sense," Walter Heerlson spoke up. "Here are two women in a highly stressful situation, then all of a sudden they just fall asleep. Quite the opposite I would expect."

Martin cleared his throat in the silence that followed.

Jim looked at him. "I think I know what you want to say, old friend. But, it's mind boggling to suspect that."

"I'm not going to argue the pro and con of that subject, but I think we should keep it in mind when all questions go unanswered," Martin replied.

"Are you two still thinking about little green men from Mars," Aaron glanced from one to the other.

"They were gray," said John. "But a score of us saw that ship and that demonstration they gave us."

"Yeah," Aaron admitted. "I saw what I saw. But was I in complete control of my faculties?"

"If you weren't, then neither were the other twenty or so that saw the same thing," said John.

"I think we should get out of here and get something to eat," said Jim.

"Good idea," said Walter. "We've got a hospital to run now that Dorothy and Laura are safe. I'll give you two a checkup before I leave."

They went up the steps to the balcony, but not before several of the women took drinks from the pool.

"Never hurts to try," said Linda. "Maybe we ought to

get checkups too. It has been several weeks since we started drinking this water."

"I'm sure Laura can take care of that," said Walter. "But I'll take any overflow."

They straggled to the main entrance, passing the stacks of supplies hoarded by Martin. Sylvia was the only one that made an effort to hurry, brushing past the others in order to stay in front. She also had to suffer the catcalls from her classmates eager to pay her back for her past cracks at their expense.

"What you sow, so shall you reap," Esther told her.

"Oh please. Quote me no quotes," Sylvia fumed. "I won't forget my 'dear friends.' My day will come."

"That's just it," said Oscar. "Your day has always been your day. And it wasn't always a nice day for those you made the butt of your remarks."

They were spared an answer as they burst out of the cave and all came up short.

The cabin, which had been built just a few yards from the cave entrance, was gone.

The treeless brush area was also gone. In its place was a forest of tall, leafy trees.

ABOUT THE AUTHOR

Peter J. Flores is a veteran who served his country during WWII. After the war, he went into Civil Service, developing work standards and computer software that would test jet aircraft engines. After retiring in 1981 he began to write stories and novels. Now, after 30 years of trying to get published, he is a first time author at age 93. When asked about his age, he merely says, "But, why stop at 93? This is just the second novel. The response to it from the public will be an indication if I should continue writing books, or whether I should confine myself to writing unprintable letters to the Editor.

Made in the USA
San Bernardino, CA
12 July 2017